C000120369

1

HIDDEN MAGIC

Fear of the Smallest Wizard

N. D. RABIN

authorHOUSE®

AuthorHouse™ UK
1663 Liberty Drive
Bloomington, IN 47403 USA
www.authorhouse.co.uk
Phone: 0800.197.4150

© 2017 N. D. RABIN. All rights reserved.

No part of this book may be reproduced, stored in a retrieval system, or
transmitted by any means without the written permission of the author.

Published by AuthorHouse 09/15/2017

ISBN: 978-1-5246-7677-3 (sc)
ISBN: 978-1-5246-7837-1 (e)

Print information available on the last page.

Any people depicted in stock imagery provided by Thinkstock are models,
and such images are being used for illustrative purposes only.
Certain stock imagery © Thinkstock.

This book is printed on acid-free paper.

Because of the dynamic nature of the Internet, any web addresses or links contained in
this book may have changed since publication and may no longer be valid. The views
expressed in this work are solely those of the author and do not necessarily reflect the
views of the publisher, and the publisher hereby disclaims any responsibility for them.

For the three little stars that twinkle in my eyes

Contents

Chapter 1: The Early Dawn

The Rutts was a quiet little road in the heart of rural North West London. It was a typical English street with a spattering of cottages lining both sides. All the cottages were slightly different due to their wooden structures shifting slightly over the years. This kind of thing could never be expected anywhere else but leafy Britain. At the centre of the road sat a school that could only have lived on this street, for the building itself was no more than an oversized cottage with two giant Tudor-style chimneys climbing out the left side. The only sign that this building was different from the others, other than it being slightly bigger, was the small playing field that came around from where the garden area would have been. It continued on and spread out to the right of the building. Over time, the building had not been big enough to house the three hundred children that went to school there, so the local authorities had built some square rooms at the back of the wide structure, leaving the pretty front to hide the ugliness of its newer growths. These rooms stretched further back than the building was wide and they all had large, plain 60s-style windows that overlooked the surrounding playing fields.

'Zachary!' the teacher hissed.

Zachary snapped back to life with a jump and looked at the teacher. 'Sorry miss,' he mumbled.

The teacher, Miss Bucket, was losing her patience with the year six class. Normally, they were a very bright and easy to manage group of eleven-year-olds, but since the thunderstorm closing in threatened the world with its loud cracks, the class and all the other students around the school were having difficulty focussing.

'Perhaps you would like to share what you find so fascinating about the storm, Zachary?' Miss Bucket suggested in a tone that did not sound like she actually wanted an answer.

'There isn't one,' Zachary stated, far too dreamily to be taken seriously.

'Don't be an idiot, Zack,' Abersheck teased with a wide grin on his face.

Abersheck was a tall, thin, kind boy with a sharp wit and an eye for mischief. He sat next to Zack in most lessons and the boys had become good friends over the last six years together.

'No seriously,' Zack seemed to brighten, 'there is thunder, but nothing else—no rain, wind, or lightning.'

'Thank you for the weather update, but perhaps you would like to focus on the reading exercises I have set?'

This also was not a question, and Zack set about the task with a severe lack of enthusiasm. He never understood the point of reading comprehension passages. 'The answers are right in front of you,' the teacher would say.

'Well, if the answer is in front of me, why do I need to point it out?' was always on his mind. He likened it to digging a hole in the earth. The hole was always there, but it needed him to excavate it for no reason at all.

English was his last lesson of the day, and time seemed to be slowing down almost to a standstill as Zachary toiled over the unfathomably dull reading work when the school bell rang and shocked him to life with welcome relief. The fog lifted, and Zachary leapt from his seat. With a few fond farewells to his classmates, he grabbed his bag and was the first one out the door. The cool spring air hit him full in the face and rushed through his long wiry hair, and Zachary's body greedily absorbed the energy of the outdoors. Just beyond the doorway of his class, Zachary stood as if he had frozen for a moment, head pointed to the sky and eyes closed, when the rush of the other children pushing past woke him. He looked up at the school gate in the distance and immediately picked out his mother instinctively. She was always there near the front. It occurred to him that she was always punctual, unlike some of the other mums. He could see her tall, slender frame. At five foot eight inches, she was just a touch taller than most of the women in the playground. She had an abundance of long, straight, dark hair and a small pretty face with an amazing smile that was able to warm the coldest of days, but today, it seemed not to reach her brown eyes. There was something behind them this afternoon, and Zack knew that it was due to the storm. Mum had been nervous about thunderstorms of any kind as far back as he could remember. She was continually obsessed with the weather and looking up at the sky. Today was no different. She kept glancing skywards like a field mouse watching out for unforeseen hunters.

Zack handed over his bag, which his mother flatly refused, stating that he was old enough already to carry it himself. He smiled inwardly, knowing that this would happen, but he had thought he would try his luck anyway. As he moved off to talk to his friends, he felt his mother's arm around him.

'Stand with me today Zacky, please,' she seemed to plead with a fearful look in her eyes, whilst still somehow wearing that big, perfect smile of hers.

'Sure, Mum.'

She pulled him close and waited for his brother and sister.

There was the usual jostling, shouting, and screeching from the throng of children mixed with parents as the end of school gathering hit its full peak with the arrival of the younger years.

Jenna often remained silent during the daily event and pondered about her never-ceasing joy at seeing mother and child reunited after only a few hours apart. She was grateful for this unrelenting happiness. She was not immune to this feeling, and when her own children came out and her heart swelled as her youngest and smallest child approached.

'Hello Jenna!' Rafi chirped, with a matching broad smile he had clearly inherited from his mother, but a look of utter mischief twinkled in his enormous brown eyes.

'Er! That's "Mummy" to you, if you don't mind, cheeky monkey,' and with that, Jenna picked him up and squeezed him tight. Zachary rolled his eyes and reached up to stroke his silky long hair.

Rafi was the baby of the family and he continued to be treated as one no matter how big he got or the amount of trouble he caused—and he caused a lot of trouble. Zachary was the antithesis of his little brother: sensible and quiet, with a relaxed manner that a monk would envy, whilst Rafi could be compared to a tightly stretched rubber band, ready to snap at any time. He seemed to challenge his size and position in the family at every turn with the energy and fervour of an Olympic athlete. Only his charm, wit, and fluttering lashes helped him escape from any wrath served upon his antics. Recently, his over-energetic antics had caused him to lose the last of his front baby teeth, leaving him all gaps and big eyes, which assisted in his continual plea of innocence from whatever it was he was guilty of.

A delicate hand touched Jenna's and she extracted Rafi from her neck and gazed upon the smaller image of herself that was Saskia, her daughter.

'Hello Mummy, I missed you!' she said as she flung both arms around Jenna's waist. At eight years old, Saskia was the only girl and was the middle child of the family. With two brothers and her father's temper, the angelic face, big blue eyes, and blond hair did not represent the inner fire that she possessed.

The reunion was complete and Jenna rushed her children out the playground and to the car with a sudden burst of energy and sharp instructions.

They lived only a few minutes away, and despite Zack's continued requests to walk on his own to school, Jenna had refused. Their house was large and white, with a red tiled roof and matching tiled canopy that surrounded the whole structure. At every corner, a thick wooden pillar held the canopy in place. This gave the house the look of a Spanish villa. The front garden was big enough for several cars and had been carefully landscaped with delicate brickwork bordering the beds and a high seven-foot wall painted white to match the main building. It subtly stated 'go away' to anyone walking by.

The car had barely come to a standstill and the front gates were gently buzzing closed when the doors burst open and the three children sprang from the car like a jack-in-the-box and raced to the front door.

'Ok, calm down,' Jenna gently guided as she opened the door and watched them fling their bags and coats on the floor to run through the entire length of the house and out into the garden. She frowned at their belongings being disregarded in such a way, but was more concerned at the increasing amount of energy they seemed to be exuding today. She looked skywards again and her frown deepened as the dark clouds overhead hinted at the storm she could smell on the wind.

The day had been dry and all three children were attempting to make the most of this, for they knew that they would never be allowed outside on a stormy day. After the usual kick about with a football that inevitably turned into 'unfair sides,' as it always would with an odd number of children, they set about playing war games. This involved the elaborate setting up of the climbing frame as a base, with the conclusion being a surprise attack from an imaginary enemy that meant the children would swing from the bars pretending to be acrobats and martial arts experts. Zachary glanced back at the house and could see his mother pretending to be busy in her bedroom overlooking the garden. He realised that people often instinctively looked at someone staring at them and he knew she was watching, probably because of the storm.

'They're coming!' screamed Rafi and pointed his tennis racket that he had named the 'baddy basher' at an invisible force heading up the garden.

'Let's get them!' Saskia pressed.

'No, get into your strike positions,' Zachary commanded and he usually got his own way.

The children all promptly invented ways of hanging on to the climbing frame, ready to strike a killer blow that in their minds left them acrobatically swinging down for the next attacker, but in reality left them awkwardly landing on the earth and making a warrior-type stance to disguise the clumsiness of their landings. Today, Rafi decided he was going to surpass his siblings and looked for the most impressive strike position. In his usual daredevil approach to life, this was instantly decided as the peak of the climbing frame. Carefully and speedily, he made his way up to the height of the familiar bell-shaped frame. The poles that made up the structure all came together at the top in a cluster held in place by one big bolt that Rafi had decided was his launch spot. He carefully placed one foot on the bolt and put the other on a pole that led to it before extending his full three foot five inches and holding his 'baddy basher' aloft with a war cry of, 'Look at me!'

The weight of the climbing frame shifted dramatically as the two other children leapt forwards to attack their imaginary foes. Rafi swayed backwards and bent over quickly to compensate, but it was not enough, and to his horror he started to fall. His feet were still on the bars, causing his small body to fall down head first and he reached out for a bar to grab, but it was too much to ask from any five-year-old. As he fell, he knew it was bad and was going to hurt, so he screamed the only comforting thought he could summon, 'Mummmmmyyyyyy!'

The human ear can pick out billions of sounds and decipher them in milliseconds. Rafi's last cry out for his mother was embroiled with panic, and instinctively, the two siblings turned to see their little brother's head come crashing to the earth.

Saskia also screamed 'Mummy!' just as the impact took place.

She immediately heard her mother's voice exclaim, 'Oh God!' even though she was not around.

The impact of Rafi's small frame hitting the ground head first seemed to happen in slow motion and the shock of the situation kicked in well ahead of the incident finishing. As Rafi's head hit the ground, and before his body came crashing down on top, causing his body to fold in two, there came a sound like a crack of thunder that emanated directly from Rafi, causing an instant flare of violent wind with his little body at the centre. A shockwave followed directly after the wind. The feeling was like a giant firework going off, except the bang was apparently a thunder crack, and it was a horrifically loud one.

It was so loud that both Zachary and Saskia cowered and held their hands over their ears as their natural reflexes caused them to crouch before the sudden violent gust pushed them over. An eerie silence and disorientation followed for the next couple of seconds. Zachary had glanced up at the window only moments before to see his mother busy in the bedroom and now she was there, almost immediately kneeling next to Rafi with a look of horror on her face. She placed her ear to his mouth and Zachary knew this was to check for his breathing. As she raised her face, he could see tears streaming down and she seemed to look older as the alarm of the situation was spreading out before him. His senses starting to come around from the blast.

'A blast came from Rafi,' he said quietly. His sister was looking at him with her face all screwed up, silently crying.

Jenna put an arm gently under Rafi's limp body and picked him up as if he were a rag doll. 'Everyone inside. Now!'

'How did you get here so quickly, Mummy?' Zachary asked in a weak, dazed voice.

'I ran, and now is not the time for questions!' snapped his mother.

Zachary knew this was impossible, but his concern for his little brother distracted him from his scepticism. As the four of them rushed down the long, messy garden, Saskia sobbed, Zachary frowned, Rafi lay unconscious, and Jenna wore a pale look of terror on her face as she scanned the skies.

Chapter 2: Time to Go

A man in a dark suit was sitting in front of a wall of screens that would make mission control at NASA seethe with envy. He jolted to life from his dreamy state as a blip on the panel directly in his line of sight glowed and grew.

'Activity!' he shouted and was immediately wide-eyed.

'Size?' quizzed a stern voice from another suit across the room.

'Big and growing.'

'Scale?'

'Started at eight on the Richter scale and is growing . . . fast!'

A group of dark-suited men and women had suddenly appeared around the one screen in the middle of the wall, watching what looked like ripples in a pond. It was as if hundreds of stones were being thrown in the same place as the outer circles got thicker and ever wider.

'What's going on?' A tall wiry man came through and the group parted to allow him access. The only difference in his attire was the black bowler hat he wore. 'Where is this?' he said with his acutely posh British accent.

'Hertfordshire, North London,' said suit number one, now fully awake.

'Targets?'

'One, sir.'

The man in the bowler hat paused and everyone hung onto his next breath. He looked up at the large audience that was now surrounding him.

'Prepare alert one!' he shouted.

The back of the big white house had two French doors at each side and a large window with a window seat in the centre. It took Jenna and James five years to build it just the way they wanted it. Its perfect symmetry, white, smooth walls, and red tiles bordered with a matching pretty canopy around its middle gave it the look of a warm, inviting home. The gardens were strewn with big, typically English bushes and trees that were the antithesis to the neatness of the main building.

The ragged quartet reached the house and entered by the left French doors next to a large apple tree. Jenna placed Rafi on the window seat whilst scouting the sky and then abruptly drew all the curtains. No one spoke and she got a flannel from the bathroom upstairs and ran cold water on it. She started to dab Rafi's small angelic face.

'Is he bleeding?' Zachary approached warily.

'No, he's just in shock.'

'Mu-Mu-Mummy,' Zachary stuttered. 'There was a bang and I'm afraid!' he exploded.

'I know darling,' the normal softness had returned to her voice. 'I'm scared too, but Daddy will be here any second and we will deal with this as a family.'

'Will he be ok?'

'Yes baby, don't worry.'

'But you look so scared and he's unconscious.'

'I am scared, and he is not unconscious. He is sleeping and will stay this way for a few days I expect.'

'Why? What is it? Was it the bang?'

She turned away from Rafi and gently drew the children close to her and placed a hand on their cheeks in a gentle caress.

'I know you are scared, my darlings, and I am too. But Mummy and Daddy will take care of you and we will all look after each other. I will answer all the questions I can later.'

The front door burst open suddenly and James came bounding in.

'What happened Jenna? Tell me everything! Where is he?'

'He's here and he's sleeping, as expected,' she shot him a look that said calm down. 'The children have all had a bit of a shock, so as Rafi's ok, why don't you give them a cuddle?'

At this warning, James's big frame enveloped the two frightened children as he knelt down on one knee and put his arms around them. Jenna found herself staring adoringly at the sight of her handsome husband with his big protective arms around her babies. At six feet two inches, with a muscular and athletic frame, Mediterranean dark looks, and chiselled features, he was enough to make most women stare for a moment. She glanced at the pencil he was wearing behind his ear and frowned, then she contemplated the slight weight he now carried around his midriff with an inwards smile at the thought of the good living they had been enjoying. The uneasy thought crept in that this life was now over.

The hug lasted a few minutes in silence and then James pulled away, looking at each of them in the eye and asking if they were ok. Both children nodded silently.

'Right! Quiet play upstairs in your rooms please. Mummy and I have some things to discuss,' he said sternly, but with a smile.

The children were acutely aware of the serious feeling in the room and obeyed without question. Once they were out the room, both children paused on the stairs and crouched low to make themselves feel silent and stealthy. They could hear the alarm in their father's voice that he had been hiding.

'How did this happen?' he snapped curtly.

'I don't know. I have been playing it through my mind over and over again.' Jenna had a much firmer grip on her emotions than her husband did, but the conversation was clearly going one way.

'How big was it?'

'Big!' her voice was stern.

'Jesus! Why weren't you watching them?'

'I can't watch them every second, James, be reasonable. I'm so tired!'

'But you're their Protector! What were you doing?' his voice was getting louder.

'I was watching them two seconds earlier and they were playing nicely. I didn't see Rafi climb to the top of the climbing frame or I would have prepared myself.'

'The top of the climbing frame! Jesus, Jenna.'

'Stop blaspheming and keep your voice down. The kids will hear.'

'Do you think anyone knows?' his voiced hushed to a low tone.

'Yes.'

'How can you be so certain?'

'Because it took every ounce of my strength to protect the children from the blast and stop the whole neighbourhood from being blown off the face of the planet!' she raised her voice at the severity of this statement.

'Jesus Christ!' he exclaimed.

'Will you stop blaspheming?' she screamed as she held her hands up to her face and began to sob uncontrollably. 'He's just a baby! How could this happen?'

'If it took all your strength to shield you, the kids, and the area, do you think he's the first?'

Jenna looked up through her swollen watery eyes in awe of what had just been said.

'He can't be . . . he's only five . . . he can't be James, he just can't be,' she sobbed.

'All your strength,' he stated rather than questioned as he examined how exhausted his normally radiant and full-of-life wife now looked.

'Yes,' came the feeble response in almost a squeak.

'Did it actually break through you?'

She nodded.

'You're certain?'

'There were car and house alarms going off far into the distance.'

'Then they are coming, and we have to go. We have to keep him safe and find out if he is the first.'

He started to move and the pair on the stairs sprang to life silently and raced up as quietly as they could. As James reached the door that led into the downstairs hall and the staircase, Jenna called out in a desperate tone.

'Where will we go?'

'Four-hundred and thirty-eight years in this world buys you a few friends—maybe one of them can help. Pack only what we need.' James said in a military tone and Jenna nodded.

Zachary raised his eyebrow and looked at his sister, whose mouth was now hanging open.

Jenna was staring at her husband as calm had finally found the family. The children were all fast asleep and she thought it must be around two in the morning. She knew she was not going to sleep tonight. Billions of thoughts and possibilities swam around her head, taking her on a rollercoaster of anxiety that swooped and preyed on her naturally relaxed demeanour.

A lone man walked up Little Bushey Lane in a dark overcoat, wrapped up tightly to defend from the cool spring wind that found its way across the open fields that were opposite the house the man was now standing outside. A quick glance up and down the long, tree-lined road and the stranger was satisfied no one was watching. Exceptionally high above the house eight figures in smart black suits and white shirts with matching black ties hung silently, motionlessly, hidden in the light sprinkling of clouds. They were all watching the house from a great distance, as if they were suspended from invisible wires, like model aeroplanes hung from an invisible ceiling. The stranger outside raised his right hand, fingers spread full and palm facing the house. He completed a wave from left to right as if sweeping a cobweb from the air in front of him.

Jenna felt the presence immediately and her senses all tensed with alarm. The fear was present in her voice, but she managed to keep calm and her voice was low and quiet.

'A Protector is outside our house,' her hand gripped James's forearm in fear.

'Then it has started,' he said impassively with a deep sigh.

As the stranger's hand completed the arc of the wave, a faint trace of a half-bubble formed gently over the house as if it were captured in a giant snow globe which faded away almost immediately. The stranger heard a person calling to a dog further up the road and slowly walked into the front drive of the white house, inside the boundary of where the half-bubble had appeared. As the dog walker strolled past, he turned to look at the house and peered straight through the dark stranger who was within arm's reach before him.

'Good evening, sir, lovely night,' said the stranger with a grin, knowing he could not be seen or heard.

The dog walker continued on, occasionally ordering the dog to hurry up.

'Shield in place,' said the stranger.

The other figures immediately appeared in eight clouds of dark swirling smoke, their bodies seemingly sucking in the gas and pulling in the molecules to quickly form a person. There were four in the front garden and four in the back garden. The one wearing a bowler hat stepped forwards and placed a hand on the front door.

'Sweep the house. I want them alive.'

Instantly, the eight figures disappeared in clouds of black smoke. The stranger was alone again in the front garden, watching the flashes of light accompanied by small bangs and pops going off like a small fireworks display making its way from room to room.

The upstairs landing was galleried and spacious. The eight sinister-looking figures closed in on the only door left closed.

'All clear sir, no contact,' said one of the figures in a low curt military tone, just above a whisper.

'They must be in there,' said bowler hat, inclining his head towards the master bedroom. 'They must be expecting us.' A smile stretched across his face. 'Remember, everyone, beyond this door is an experienced and powerful Warrior with his Protector. Take no chances. On my mark.' He held aloft three fingers and counted them all down to one finger, whilst all eight figures closed in on the door.

The door was blown away by an invisible force with such strength that it crashed through the opposite window, missing the giant bed that lay just below its trajectory.

The room was empty. A small note that had been laid out on the perfectly made king-sized bed fluttered in the fresh spring wind that now circled the room from the giant hole that represented the place where the window use to be. The note read:

Nice hat!

James pulled the car into the service station's long-haul car park and parked in the most remote part he could find. He turned to look at his three sleeping babies in the back seat and then smiled at Jenna.

'Finally! They're asleep,' he mused.

'Our house has been taken,' Jenna said quietly. 'I sensed his anger at your note.'

'I just want them to know we are a force to reckon with. That stunt will go around the network like wildfire and reach those outside of the organisation who have now heard about Rafi. Consider it a warning shot.' He frowned deeply at this last statement and he left it hanging in the air for a moment. 'Back in ten minutes.' He leaned over and kissed Jenna full on the lips and disappeared into a cloud of black smoke.

Fifteen minutes later, a gentle swishing noise and a small cloud of swirling black smoke signified his return. He held his hand palm up at head height. In it was a large key attached to a larger piece of leather with gold letters on it. It read:

Penthouse Garden Suite

He tilted his head to the side and a wry smile stretched across his face as he handed the key to Jenna. She tilted her head to read the writing and raised an eyebrow.

'Inconspicuous,' she said with more than a hint of sarcasm.

'Well, our cover has been blown, so I figured we should go forwards in style,' he shrugged.

They joined hands and leaned over into the back seats. James reached out and took Zachary's hand and moved it over to join with Saskia's. Jenna held Rafi's hand and internally noted that he was too hot and thought he must have a temperature. All five figures disappeared in a cloud of black swirling smoke as the car gently rocked.

Chapter 3: The Old Man

Zachary tried to open his eyes, but found that they were fighting him to stay asleep. He could hear the low level noise of his father talking to someone nearby and then could pick out his mother's response.

The room was very bright. Sunlight was streaming in from somewhere and Zachary could feel a cool breeze on his face. His body was exceptionally comfortable and he was snug inside a heavy, white, luxurious duvet. His head was on a matching pillow of equal comfort, and when he raised it beyond the warm cocoon he was in, he could see the bed spread beyond those of normal dimensions. His brother and sister were on either side of him, sleeping soundly.

As Zachary turned his head to take in his surroundings, he started to gape at the sheer opulence and openness of the large white and gold room. The bed was enormous and could easily hold another three or four people aside from him and his siblings. It had a four-poster frame with thin white linen curtains gently swaying in the breeze that was blowing in from the far side of the room, where two grand golden doors were open and bordered with matching white linen curtains. Around the room were oversized pieces of ornate golden furniture with white linen coverings. Altogether, the place felt like a palace where perhaps the queen of England might stay. Slowly and heavily, he dragged himself out of bed, being careful not to disturb anyone, and padded across to the balcony doors which were facing the bed and led out into the sunlight. He held his hand up to his eyes in a semi-salute to shield himself from the bright white sun pouring down on him.

'Good morning, handsome,' came his mother's voice. Zachary turned to the right to see that the balcony stretched far beyond the room he was in—much further along the building— and had matching doors into other rooms. His parents were sitting at a white wrought iron table with matching chairs with oversized cushions on them. They had an assortment of breakfast foods and drinks on the table, all presented in white bone china and silver cutlery that matched the whole palatial experience. They were wearing thick white bath robes with the words *'Hotel Monasterio'* inscribed across the left part of the chest area.

Jenna had her hair in a ponytail and she was playing with the crystal necklace James had given to her when they first met, which she never took off. James had peeled the top of his robe off and was basking in the sunshine. Zachary could see that even now he was wearing a pencil behind his ear. Zachary couldn't remember seeing him without it. Dad always said, 'You never know when you will need to write something down,' whenever someone challenged him about it. Zachary thought that they both looked like they belonged in a catalogue, given their attire and the surroundings.

He looked to the left, and it was then that he noticed the view. Just beyond the balcony was a sprawling city that stretched far out into the distance, where giant mountains seemed to surround and fortify it. All the buildings were the same height, with white walls and dark, deep red tiles on the rooftops. They were packed so tightly together that it was hard to believe anything could pass between them. The view he had was of one side of the city from a hilltop. The perfectly matching buildings gave him the feeling that he was looking at a model village, and that he could become a giant amongst the inhabitants by stepping over the balcony edge. In the forefront of the view was a square with a large fountain and a large, squat building with two giant bell towers that stood out amongst the matching architecture of the other buildings. Zachary thought this must be a cathedral of some kind.

'Blimey! Where are we?'

'Peru!' Jenna said with a beaming smile. 'Do you like the view? We thought that given the trauma of yesterday, we would go on a spontaneous trip and chillax for a bit in the sunshine.'

'How did we get here?' Zachary frowned as he tried to recall their journey.

'Well, we drove to the airport and you guys fell asleep on the way. Your poor father had to ferry you all on the trolley all the way to the plane.'

'And from the airport to the hotel,' James added jovially.

'We stayed asleep the whole time?' Zachary quizzed.

'Yep,' they both chirped.

'I'm eleven years old right?'

'Yes,' said Jenna, starting to frown.

'That makes me young—not an idiot. Now, are you going to tell me what's going and why we are here and why Rafi exploded yesterday and how we got here and all that? Or shall we continue to pretend I'm an idiot?' He was starting to become irate and upset.

'SHH-shh-shh, darling,' Jenna leapt up and wrapped her arms around him. As she did this, she shot James a look that he understood immediately to mean: *tell him . . . please.*

James placed the coffee he was drinking down on the table and uncrossed his legs whilst leaning forward. His hands reached out and Zachary moved out of his mother's all-encompassing hold to place both his hands in his father's. James gazed into his son's big brown eyes and he momentarily despaired at the conversation he knew was imminent and premature in his version of how his children's lives should have been.

'There is no easy way to say this, so I guess I'll just say it. We are wizards,' he left it hanging out there for a second. 'Some people call us magicians, oracles, miracle makers. . . .'

'Witches?' Jenna piped in with her eyebrows raised.

'Yes, witches, sorcerers, conjurers—we have been known as many things over the centuries, but I think I am most comfortable with the name "wizard."'

'Blimey!' a small voice squeaked from behind the curtains and the big blue eyes and long flowing blond hair of Saskia came into view.

'Brilliant,' James rolled his eyes at Jenna in a gesture of exasperation, 'at what point did you start eavesdropping, young lady?'

'Erm, when you said we were in Peru, I think.' Saskia now had her head tilted down with eyes wide staring up, trying to make herself look as innocent as possible.

'Brilliant,' James repeated, 'well, I guess there is no point in saying it twice.'

'Shall I wake Rafi?' Saskia asked brightly.

'It's going to take a little more than you to do that, honey,' Jenna said with comfort in her voice.

James faced both his children and drew them close.

'I'm going to tell you some stuff now and I will try and answer all of your questions as best I can, but I don't know all the answers and that may be difficult for you to take in,' he began and the children both nodded. 'The explosion that came from Rafi yesterday was called a "Dawn", and it signified a change in his body. He is changing and growing in ways that will make your head spin.'

'Changing how?'

'His brain is waking up to new things he will be able to do. You see, most people go through life only using around ten percent of their brain and Rafi's brain has just been jolted into a new life where some parts have been stirred and woken up. That's why it's called a "Dawn" or sometimes the "Crack of Dawn".'

'Will it happen to me?' asked Zachary.

'Yes, I fully expect that you and your sister will follow shortly. In fact, your close proximity to Rafi's Dawn means that you are both unstable and likely to crack at any impact or shock.'

Saskia's eyebrows raised high and tears came into her eyes.

'Will it hurt?' she said softly.

'No baby, you won't feel a thing, but I fear for those around you.' He shot a look at Jenna. 'Rafi's Dawn was about the biggest I have ever heard of and it took all of your mother's strength to stop half of our town from being blown off the planet. Normally, these things are more like . . . er . . . a firecracker going off, but Rafi's Dawn,' he blew out a soft whistle, 'crikey!' he said shaking his head.

'How did Mummy protect us?' Zachary looked at his mother.

'Well, scientifically speaking, our brains have been awakened in parts that are normally dormant in most people. "Dormant" means "sleeping",' he directed the latter comment at Saskia, who was looking puzzled, 'and this has given us the ability to control matter, you know, molecules and atoms: the stuff, stuff is made up of. It's an incredible ability and one that must be used with great care. Think about it: if you can control molecules, you can draw them in and,' he paused for effect, 'make things.' He held his hand in front of the children's eyes, palm up, and they could see a small swirl of white mist building up until the small fog cleared and a glass of water sat in his palm. 'Drink?' he offered the kids. Zachary took the glass with his mouth wide open and completely in shock. Jenna leaned forwards and faced the children.

'If you understand how things are made up or at least how you have felt them to be made up, you can conjure them, like Daddy just did.' She sat upright. 'But if you feel where they are, you can just as easily move them.' She raised her right hand and clicked her fingers. The glass immediately disappeared from Zachary's hand and into her own. She clicked again and the glass floated from her hand to directly in front of Saskia's head. She picked the glass out of the air with a grin. 'Or perhaps understanding the matter or object could mean thinking about its state.'

'State?' said Zachary.

'Yes,' James interjected now, thoroughly enjoying the conversation, 'taste it. Is it hot, cold, or warm?'

Zachary took the glass from his sister and drank a sip.

'Cold.'

'How do we make it hot?' said James. 'It's just about making the water molecules move faster, in essence,' and he waved his hand at the glass, and immediately, the water started to bubble violently.

'Aaah!' Zachary shrieked and dropped the glass, which smashed into thousands of pieces on the floor. James leapt up and grabbed his hand, turning it over to look at the red, raw, burnt fingertips on his son.

'I'm so sorry, sunshine, but think about it. When your skin is burnt and hot, that's just the current state of the matter that makes you, you.' Jenna leaned in and enclosed his little hand between both of hers. There was a small glow of light and Zachary felt like his hand was under a small sun lamp momentarily.

'You see? All better,' Jenna showed the hand to Saskia and she nodded. 'Or do you really see?' James smiled, knowing what was coming next. Jenna was inches from her daughter, and with Zachary's hand in hers, slowly, their image started to wave and blur to Saskia and James. Then it faded out completely. Saskia's mouth hung open.

'Mummy?' she whispered.

'Yes, my lovely girl?' the voice came directly into her ear, as if Jenna were mere inches from her head, which she was. Saskia turned sharply and James watched as she and Zachary re-materialised in the opposite direction from the one Saskia was now looking at.

'You see, if you feel and understand your surroundings, then perhaps you can imitate them, so that others can't see you,' Jenna said, wearing a big smile, 'like a chameleon—only better.'

'What else can you do? And when can I do it?' Zachary was very excited.

'Easy tiger,' said James, 'all in good time. You will need to have your own Dawn first, my son, and that will make you very tired. After that comes years and years of training, understanding and discipline. The list of boring stuff that comes first is long.' James ruffled his hair.

'How old are you, Daddy?' asked Saskia.

'Hmm, now, why would you ask a question like that?' James's lips narrowed and he looked at Jenna, who offered him centre stage with a sweeping hand gesture.

'No reason.'

'Little people should not eavesdrop quite so much,' he said with a serious note. 'Well, if you must know, I am thirty-eight . . . plus a few years.'

'How many is a few?'

'Well, I'm 438 to be exact.' Both children's jaws dropped. A long pause followed.

'How old are you Mummy?' asked Saskia.

'Thirty-seven, my darling,' she said with a smile.

'Thirty-seven plus how many?'

'Just plain old boring "thirty-seven" I'm afraid. I am a mere baby compared to your father.'

'Ha! Boring is right,' James said playfully.

'Watch it you! Or I'll turn you into a frog.' The children's mouths hung open again and they looked at their mother in awe. 'I was just kidding' she said and began to giggle.

'Dad, you must know so much. Where were you born?' Zachary was getting excited again.

'I was born in 1574, in an exceptionally small cottage near the famous Temple Church close to the River Thames in London. My mother was a lovely, caring lady, but I never knew my father.' He trailed off and sadness reached his eyes. 'Fortunately, the church had recently become governed by the Crown again. It all belonged to Queen Elizabeth the first!' he said loudly, 'and my mother was able to get help from the priests in the church the night I was born. So, yes, I have seen quite a lot, but we are going out soon, so that's enough for now.'

'What! I have a million questions,' said Zachary.

'And I have a million answers, but that's enough for now apart from one last thing.' James's face became very serious and he drew the children close again. 'History has taught us many things, but one lesson stands out amongst them all. That lesson is that there is danger for us and our kind when normal people know of our existence. You must not tell anyone—ever—about this. It would bring danger to us all. Do you understand?' Both children nodded. 'Right then, get dressed!' he snapped.

'Where are we going?' asked Zachary.

'To meet a friend. We need to find out what's going on with Rafi, in particular, why he nearly blew us all to smithereens.' He smiled at this comment either due to nervousness or the influence from his youngest son's typical behaviour. 'You see, in 438 years, you get to know a few people who know a few things.' He winked at the children.

Chapter 4: The Even Older Friend

The kids got dressed in the clothes they wore the previous day and James wrapped a blanket around himself to form a baby harness into which he placed Rafi, who was still fast asleep. Rafi snorted and snored loudly at being moved and everyone giggled. They all left the room in single file and Jenna called from the rear, 'We all need new clothes and some toiletries.'

'We can get all that at the market,' James said. 'Everything we need will be there,' and he smiled a knowing smile, as if he were keeping a secret.

They entered the spacious, ostentatious hotel lobby and Zachary was once again reminded of Buckingham Palace, which he had visited on a school trip. A white Mercedes taxi was waiting for them outside, and as James opened the doors for his family, he tipped the doorman and glanced up and down the road, up at the sky, and then looked at Jenna, who subtly nodded before entering the car.

'Plaza de Armas, *por favor*' said James as he entered the front seat of the car with Rafi still strapped to his front.

The journey took them through very narrow bumpy roads where people wearing big brimmed hats and what looked like blankets as capes had to dart out of the way to let the car pass. They arrived in less than ten minutes at the giant square Zachary had seen from the hotel balcony and pulled up alongside the fountain. James paid the taxi driver and stepped out. He walked around the car, surveyed the area, and paused before letting Jenna out first. She held the children back for a moment before helping them out. The miniature cathedral Zachary had seen from the balcony now looked enormous, and he could see the many bells in the giant towers and the giant fortified front door, which had a smaller open door within it, presumably to let normal-sized people through. Zachary wondered who was big enough to use the giant entrance. The family walked to the side of the square towards a large building held up by many pillars with multiple rooftops layered over each other, but no walls. The sign above the entrance read 'San Pedro Market'.

'Here we are kids, the multicultural delight of San Pedro Market,' James said with a grin. 'You know this place has been here for hundreds of years in one form or another.' He bent low and whispered in the nervous-looking Saskia's ear, 'I would know.' He winked at her and she smiled.

'Why are we here, Dad?' asked Zachary, and before he could get an answer, the full impact of the market took all conversation away. Zachary had never seen so many colours in one place. It was as if someone had captured a rainbow and spread it out before them. There were people standing in front of stands that sold all kinds of brightly coloured and pungent vegetables, flowers, powders, animals—the list was endless. The family walked through in silence until Saskia noticed a big man in a white shirt. He was smiling at her with what few teeth he had left and waving his hands to present his goods, which looked like a large, gruesome pile of donkey noses and mouths.

'Daddy!' Saskia squeaked and hugged James's leg tightly, burying her face into his side and pointing in the general direction of the man. James looked over and smiled down at his daughter.

'Hmm, roast donkey snouts,' he said licking his lips, 'delicious. Don't knock it until you've tried it, kiddo.'

'That's disgusting, Dad,' she said, peeling herself away from him with a look of disgust, but it was clear that a smile was beginning to grow.

'Hey, if you're hungry enough, you'll eat anything. There wasn't always a supermarket around, you know.'

They continued through the market and the family started to relax and take it all in. The sellers were exceptionally friendly and used the international language of miming to communicate with the children and their parents.

The kids had gathered around a woman selling pizza as a man tried to convince Jenna she definitely needed a wooden spoon from his giant assortment of wooden cutlery. A man approached selling rugs, and remarkably, he was carrying several large ones over his hunched shoulders, much to the surprise of the kids. James bent down and engaged the man in a low conversation in a language that Jenna recognised as Spanish. She had learnt Spanish in school, but lack of use had made her rusty, whereas James was now speaking the language fluently.

'Daddy speaks Spanish?' Saskia whispered to her mother.

'And German, Italian, French—in fact, most languages except Mandarin.'

'Mandarin?' Saskia frowned.

'It's Chinese, or one dialect of it. He has had a few years to learn them.' She nudged her daughter. 'Don't mention the Mandarin. He's a bit touchy about it.' They giggled.

James thanked the man and then looked deeper into the market where the man had pointed.

'This way,' he announced. 'He is here,' he whispered into Jenna's ear.

They walked deeper and deeper into the market and the outside world seemed to disappear. People were bustling everywhere and it was hard to squeeze through the throng at points. It seemed to Zachary that the whole city had turned out today, and that all the tourists had come to witness the occasion. Cameras flashed at the bright stands and around the performers who now littered the wider walkways and few open spaces. There were sword swallowers, musicians playing instruments he had never seen, and even snake charmers to distract people from the incredible stalls and sellers calling out their wares in shouts and squawks.

The children led the way towards a stand with all kinds of masks on it and were starting to pick them up and show how silly they looked to each other. As Jenna approached them, she stopped dead in her tracks and looked around with sharp urgent turns of her head. James walked up behind her.

'What is it?'

'They are here. I can feel them and their desire to find us. We aren't safe.'

'I'm ready, but can you shield us?'

'For a period, yes, but if they see us, then you'll have to be quick.' She shot him a warning look.

'Ok, take Rafi from me. Let's find him and get out of here. Come on kids, put them down and let's move on.' James guided them on with his hands. As they walked on, Saskia shot one last longing look at the princess mask she had been trying on a moment ago, and then she noticed him.

At seven foot two inches tall, with a bald head covered with tattoos that stretched down over half his face and a physique that would make any professional wrestler feel envious, Saskia knew this man was a giant from a fairy tale. The fear of this impossible human being before her did not come only from his size, but also from the intense stare that he was giving her father. Saskia's brain had been overloaded with terror, stemming the scream that was now swelling in her stomach.

The giant suddenly sprang to life, awakening from his gawking. He moved with impossible strides that covered the twenty feet between them in just a few steps. Saskia's face stretched into awe combined with horror as she watched him block out the sunlight with his gigantic form. He reached over the family to grab her father by his shoulders, doing so from behind in what appeared to be slow motion. Saskia craned her head so far back to see him that it felt like she might fall over.

Her father shrank down as the giant grabbed his shoulders, causing him to reach lower and bend over, and what happened next made her eyebrows rise so high that they practically met her hairline. James sprang up from his crouch like a coiled spring suddenly released. He leapt into a backwards somersault using the giant's shoulders as hand rests and completed a handstand with his arms outstretched over the giant's head. As he completed the arc of his somersault, he collapsed down behind the giant, using his weight and a knee in the back to leverage the massive weight off balance and pull him down into a seated position on the floor with his legs outstretched before him. The giant was now like a large toy figure that had been placed into an unnatural position for an adult. Her father had manoeuvred his arms into a chokehold around the giant's massive neck and Saskia could see that he was cutting the air supply from the shocked would-be attacker.

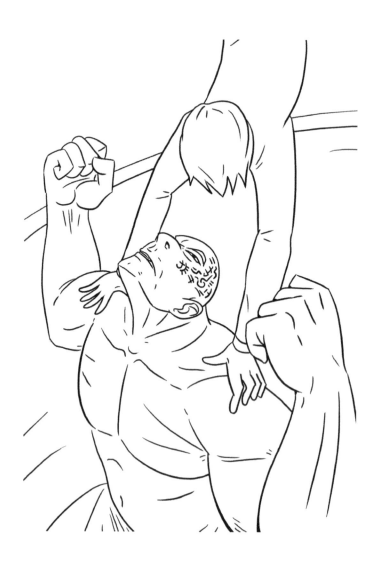

'Hello, old man,' James said into the giant's ear. He let go and circled around to the front of the giant and offered him a hand up.

'Ha!' the giant bellowed with a large toothy grin and the whole family collectively let out the breath they had been holding.

The two men gripped each other's forearms and the giant pulled against James to help himself to his feet. The crowd that had paused beside the sudden struggle had now started to move on.

'Blimey, Gwion! I was expecting something a little more . . . erm . . . inconspicuous,' James exclaimed as the massive man stretched out to his full height before him.

'Well, I'm just hiding in plain sight. It's the best way.' Gwion's deep booming voice matched his appearance. He stepped back and took in the sight of James with a hand raised up to his chin and a finger on his lip. 'Is it really you, old friend?' he said with disbelief in his voice. 'It's been so long! How have you been?' he smiled.

James grabbed the giant with both hands about his face, squashing in his cheeks to reveal his perfectly white teeth. 'I see you got your teeth fixed,' he said, moving the giant's head left and right.

'Wonders of modern medicine,' he smiled again and reached forwards suddenly to bear hug James making him look like a child within his massive frame. The men paused for a moment and then Gwion placed James down and bellowed, 'I hear you took a wife, is it true?'

At this, Jenna stepped forwards and held her hand out.

'Hello Gwion, I'm Jenna, lovely to finally meet you. I have heard so much.'

Gwion took a step back, making Jenna feel awkward and sized her up for a moment, leaving her hanging there. Then he tilted his head sideways and spoke out the corner of his mouth towards James in a staged whisper that was completely audible to everyone.

'Nice work, she's looovely.' He stretched the last words out, causing Jenna to flush bright crimson and reached out to take her hand and shook it, making Jenna struggle to stay on her feet.

'And these are my children.' James started by pointing at the two dumbstruck kids standing beside their mother and then pointing to the small one still wrapped in a sling behind Jenna.

'Well, stone me, you have been busy.' He paused. 'There must be trouble, though, or you wouldn't be here looking for me.'

'I need to talk to you somewhere private.'

'Sure, I have some introductions of my own to make,' Gwion said and opened his massive arms to guide the family in the direction he had come from, further into the market's heart.

'Anyone tired?' He directed this question towards the children.

'My feet hurt,' said Saskia, hiding most of her body from Gwion behind her mother as they walked.

'Need a lift?' he smiled and crouched down and waited, beckoning the children over with his oversized arms. Zachary was the first over and Gwion picked him up like rag doll and placed his bottom on one of his shoulders. Then Gwion tilted his head to one side. 'You coming?' he asked, smiling at Saskia, who raised one eyebrow and then slowly peeled herself from her mother's leg. As she was lifted to his shoulder, she wondered if this was what her classroom hamster felt like whenever it was picked up by one of the children.

'Let's go!' bellowed Gwion, and he stood to his full height, making the children feel like they were rising in an elevator. They walked on deeper and deeper into the market, and from nearly ten feet up, the kids could see the massive market sprawling out before them. Anything from this unusual angle would look strange, but the marketplace with all its exotic sights was captivating. The market was divided into sections where food, livestock, spices, clothing, and many other things were being sold, but it was the colour of the spice and clothing areas that stood out. Zachary grimaced at some of the scary food varieties being offered and felt sorry for the livestock as they passed by.

Finally, they reached a section where all the stalls were selling furniture. They stopped before an elaborate stand of incredible hand carved chairs and tables that all appeared to be suitable for someone of Gwion's size. Zachary could see two men working behind a table on its side at the back of the display and Gwion called out, 'Boys, boys, come at once! I have someone I want you to meet.'

Zachary had thought they were standing already, but it was immediately clear that these two men were Gwion's sons. They looked up after hearing the familiar voice and stood to their full height. Both were slightly shorter than Gwion and had far fewer muscles, making them look more like teenage versions of him with thick mops of hair on their heads.

'James, Jenna, these are my sons, Grublidblach and Patrick.' Saskia tried desperately to stifle a giggle at the first boy's name, to which he frowned and blushed. Patrick was very dark skinned, with dark hair and thick lines on his forehead making him look very serious. Grublidblach was extremely pale and had a thin smiling face with bright blonde hair.

'Call me Grub,' he said, shooting a distasteful look at his father in obvious disgust at his name.

'Two more to add to the clan,' said James. 'How many is that now?'

'Thirty-seven if you count the ones we lost in battle.'

'Well, I think these two are the biggest so far. Have they been trained yet?'

The boys shifted on their feet uncomfortably at being discussed in this way in front their father.

'Yes, they have!' he beamed proudly. 'Grub just finished and Patrick has one more year—if he passes,' and he nudged his son, who shifted again to the other foot.

'Hmm, good to know.'

'Yes, it is, especially with the number of agents around today, which I'm guessing has something to do with you and this visit?'

'Suits?'

'Nah! Plain clothes, but they may as well be wearing suits. They stand out like tourists,' he said and laughed.

'Yep, where's Nellie? We need to talk.'

'She won't come here—hates it. She runs the stand at the Lost City Market.'

'It's her I came to see.'

'Charming, good to see you too mate!'

'Gwion, this is serious.'

'Boys, I think the children would love to see the handmade toys just over there for a few minutes.'

Jenna shot James a look of fear.

'Relax!' said Gwion. 'You are in safe hands. You can trust me.' He caught his sons' eyes, 'stay close and be aware.' The boys nodded and Grub gestured towards the direction Gwion had pointed. Gwion placed his giant hands around the waist of each child on his shoulders, gently lifted them off, and guided them towards their mother.

'Here, let me have Rafi.' Jenna lifted the sling off and kissed the sleeping child's head before strapping him to James's back.

Jenna watched as James and Gwion immediately engaged in a very serious discussion that made James's arms wave around animatedly as she walked away. She was soon distracted by the sellers offering her anything and everything she could ever desire. The children yelped and gawped at the incredible toys that the Peruvian locals had made. Jenna was reminded of the toys her parents had played with. There were windup and clockwork figures whizzing and whirring all over the place. All were beautifully made and came in bright colours, and it seemed that every one of those toys they came across was more ingenious than the next. It took great effort for Jenna to force the children to put them down and break away from the engaging merchants who had already started lowering their prices at the mere sign of any interest from the family.

As they darted from stall to stall, Grub and Patrick walked just behind the family in silence. Jenna tried several times to start a conversation, but the boys seemed to be shy and too awkward to speak with her. They were more content looking around over the heads of the people around them.

'Pretty crystals for a pretty lady!' called a merchant from two stands away.

This caught Jenna's attention and she knew that the man had noticed the elaborate crystal she always wore around her neck. Immediately, she strolled over to the stall, trying not to look too eager.

'I do good price for such a pretty lady,' he pitched as he limped in her direction, leaning heavily on an ugly iron walking stick. He was a short man with thick dark hair and Mediterranean colouring who was in need of a good wash. He was wearing a light beige suit that had seen better days and had a creepy demeanour that Jenna put down to his hunger for sales.

The children followed with Grub and Patrick close behind. The merchant eyed up the two giant boys. Jenna caught him glancing and he looked back at her, smiling nervously.

'You have an eye for good crystals, don't you?' said the merchant, gesturing towards the crystal around her neck and then to his stall.

'Hmm, they are lovely,' Jenna mumbled out of politeness, but she was not impressed as they were cheap, poor quality crystals that were not of much use to her. As she started to walk away, the merchant's desperation came out in his voice.

'Today, I will do a special offer: buy two and get one absolutely free!' he beckoned her over with his hands. 'You see, one for each of your children.' He smiled.

The merchant realized his mistake immediately as a look of recognition and fear flashed in Jenna's eyes. She only had two of her children with her, so how could he have known that she had three children? They both reacted with incredible speed, Jenna reaching for the crystal around her neck and the merchant raising the walking stick to point it at her. She pushed the necklace out in front of her, palm first, towards the seller and there was a bright flash of light and a loud crack in the air. The seller, encumbered by his weakened leg, had only raised his stick halfway up when the force hit him with a loud explosion, sending him flying into his stall accompanied by the sound of shattering glass splinters hitting the ground. The market stood silent for a moment, and then from somewhere, a woman screamed and people started to run away in panic in all directions. The merchant quickly got back on his feet, and then he wiped away the blood trickling down his face and rushed towards Jenna, who stood in shock at the destruction she had just caused.

Grub and Patrick had grabbed the two children, shielding them from whatever was coming next and Grub raised his tree trunk leg out in a forwards kick to block the merchant from attacking. The merchant tapped the giant foot with his walking stick, which was now stretched out before him, like a vicious conductor and Grub was flipped over like a toy. He was a few feet away from Jenna, who was still in shock, when a soft pop was heard in the air and a whirlwind of black smoke appeared before him, thwarting his attack. The merchant backed up immediately upon seeing James burst from the smoke holding a large wooden staff that was as tall as he was and as thick as the handle of a tennis racket.

'You!' said James with distaste in his voice.

'We just want to talk. We only want to talk. There is no danger here,' the assailant said as he grovelled.

'You're underestimating me, because I see plenty of danger here for you, Teivel.' James puffed out his chest and snarled at the merchant, who cowered.

'Was that the source of the gigantic Dawn?' said the merchant, pointing to the child on James's back and peering over to get a better look. 'He's so young. He must surely be the first to return.' He paused at the thought. 'How will you protect him? How will you protect yourselves?' he said, getting excited, 'You need us!'

'Now, you listen to me, Teivel, you won't take me or my family, ever! Even if it means another war!'

'A war?' Teivel smirked, 'You against the whole corporation? Give it up now before someone gets hurt. We just want to talk.'

'You can tell Hadrian I have faced worse odds before and won,' James snarled. 'Or perhaps you need another reminder? How's the leg?'

Teivel's mouth flickered into a snarl at this last comment and he stood upright. 'Take them now!' he screamed in a high-pitched, desperate wail. All at once, men and woman appeared on all sides of the family. Most were holding sticks that reminded Zachary of magic wands, but they were all different sizes, colours, and textures. The rest were holding objects like rocks or marbles in much the same way as his mother had held out her crystal, except this time they were all pointed towards him and his family. He wondered how much the explosion he had just seen hurt. The giant boys had positioned themselves between the new arrivals and the family. Together with James, they formed a triangle around Jenna and the children.

'Not today,' whispered James as he swiped his staff in the air and spun it over his head, causing another boom in the now-silent marketplace. Jenna had heard the signal from James in her head before he reacted and she felt the power of the wizards holding them there dissipate immediately with the explosion. In a cloud of black smoke, they were transported back to the hotel suite, breathless and shocked.

James rounded on Jenna, who was still and exhausted from shifting the whole family plus two giants so quickly.

'Can they see us!' he said urgently. She did not react. 'Jenna,' he grabbed her and shook her slightly, 'can they see us? Are they coming?' He held his staff out, ready to react.

'No, they can't see us. We are safe,' she whispered breathlessly.

James lowered his staff and breathed out a long sigh. The giant boys lowered their arms and moved out from their protective positions and then they looked at James.

'Nice move,' said Patrick.

'Thanks,' said James, 'sorry to have gotten you involved.'

'You kidding!' said Grub with a big smile. 'That's the most action I have ever had. These days, the tests are all "health and safety". There's practically no real danger for a Warrior to face, at all.'

'Really? And your dad's ok with that?'

'Nah,' Patrick pitched in, 'he tries to take us out all the time, but he's old and slow.' Both the boys laughed.

'Is he really slow?' James frowned and looked a little sad.

'Yeah, so we had better get back and make sure he's ok.'

'Sure,' James said glumly.

'Don't worry,' Grub nudged James, 'you have a few years before you're his age.'

'Yeah, still life in the old boy yet,' Patrick teased.

Suddenly, two large swirls of black smoke wound up from the floor accompanied by two pops, and the boys were gone.

Chapter 5: A Brief History of Magic

'What was that?' Zachary exclaimed.

'Which bit?' James asked calmly.

'All of it. The stick-thingy,' he pointed to James's staff, 'Mummy shooting explosions out of her necklace, those people in the market . . .'

'. . . That nasty man, Evil,' Saskia pitched in.

'His name is "Teivel,"' James said with a smile.

'And how did we suddenly get back here?' Zachary's voice was extremely high-pitched now.

'Slow down, slow down,' James put his arms around the children. 'I think that perhaps a little Q&A is in order.'

'Q&A?' asked Saskia.

'Questions and answers,' said Jenna soothingly, now coming back to her normal self.

'Let's order up some food and chat,' said James, and he picked up the golden telephone on the ornate table near him.

'Hello, is this room service? Excellent! I would like two of everything on the kid's menu, one tuna niçoise salad with extra dressing, one rib eye steak, bloody, four portions of your finest cheesecake, and four glasses of lemonade please.'

Zachary raised an eyebrow and smiled at his sister. James sat down on one of the large plump sofas and patted the seats next to him, which signified that the children should sit there. Jenna placed Rafi on the bed in the main bedroom and came back in.

'Right, where do you want to start?'

'What's that?' Zachary pointed to the staff.

'What, this?' James held the staff out before him and twisted it so that it lay horizontally in the air. The wooden fibres that were tightly wound together to make up the staff suddenly became loose and the wooden pole started to constrict. Within a few seconds, it was no more than a pencil and James placed it behind his ear. 'This is my pencil,' James said smiling. The children's mouths hung open. 'This pencil, and Mummy's necklace, are our elements.'

'What are elements?' Saskia questioned.

'Elements are the materials that make up solid objects, like wood, crystal, rock, and stone, for example—the stuff, stuff is made off. All wizards have two elements in their blueprint, and no one knows why they are what they are or how you get a specific type. One element channels your power, like wood for me, or oak, to be exact. Using a simple piece of oak in my hands, my power can be channelled and focussed into an area. Otherwise, it would spread out all over the place and I would only be able to do small things or maybe big splodges of uncontrolled magic.' Both the children were frowning. 'Ok, try this. You know a magnifying glass?' The children nodded. 'What happens when you try and harness the sun's light through it?'

'It gets hot underneath,' said Zachary.

'Right! But if you don't focus the beam, then the light you are channelling is large and won't burn anything. But if you focus the beam . . .'

'. . . It burns!' Saskia added eagerly.

'You got it.' James was smiling. 'So a wizard's element is like a magnifying glass for magic. Mine is oak and Mummy's is crystal.'

'Will mine be crystal?' Saskia asked, longingly looking at her mother's necklace.

'Maybe,' said Jenna, placing an arm around the little girl.

'What does the other element do? You said that we all have two,' Zachary asked, jumping back into the conversation.

'Good question! The other is the most fearful of all for a wizard, although it can be used to help others. Have you ever heard the scientific phrase, "For every reaction, there is an equal and opposite reaction"?' Both children shook their heads. 'Well, what that means is that for everything that happens, there is a consequence. An example is how out of breath and tired Mummy was when we got back to the hotel. She teleported seven people across a city and it drained her energy. This is the same with your elements: one will channel your powers and the other will draw them away from you.'

'Like Superman and kryptonite?' said Zachary.

'Kind of,' Jenna said in a calmer voice than the rest, 'except the magic gets held in the element like a battery. This can be used by wizards to help others.'

'What! You could give me your power?' Zachary said overexcitedly.

'Through my second element, you could hold my power and channel it through your first element, yes.'

'How can I help someone with my second element?' asked Saskia and Jenna looked at her with adoration, knowing that her daughter loved to help others.

'You see, she is a born Healer,' Jenna said to James. 'All wizards have the same abilities,' she began. 'Some are more or less powerful than others, but we can all do the same things; it's knowing how to do them that's the hard bit. Some are good at pushing molecules about, which if they focus makes them good at flying by forcing objects, including themselves, around.'

'Or something like my wooden staff or even my fists,' James interjected.

'Quite,' Jenna continued, 'these wizards are known as Warriors.'

'Cool.' said Zachary 'Are you a Warrior, Daddy?'

'Yep,' James said proudly, puffing out his chest, 'I can increase my speed and put force behind anything I move or even build up a shield of energy before my own fist as it flies into a baddy!'

'Others can move and feel molecules and matter, drawing them in to make bigger objects, like the glass of water the other day, but bigger—much bigger. These wizards have been called "Conjurers" for centuries.'

'Big objects like what?' Zachary quizzed.

'Like stone giants or sea serpents to frighten people or just plain old big boulders to fall on your enemy. Ha! I've seen a few of those. They're nothing me and my wand can't obliterate.'

'Or perhaps water where people are thirsty or wood where people need a fire,' Jenna interjected, shooting James a look of agitation.

'Yes, of course you are right, darling. Conjurers can do incredibly helpful things and they are especially good at teleporting because it's all about moving matter, which is their speciality.'

'And then, there are my favourite wizards, Healers. They can bind matter together and are usually particularly good with living organisms. These people are littered throughout history as miracle-makers, often not knowing how they accomplished their great feats, but those who have learned to use their elements to harness this type of power can do incredible good.'

'I hope I'm a Healer. What kind of wizard are you, Mummy?' asked Saskia.

'I am a Protector.' Jenna beamed. Saskia smiled at her mother at this thought, though she had no idea what this meant. 'I can form barriers against all kinds of energy and forces. I can feel people's emotions and senses and block them out.'

'Like a force field?' Saskia asked.

'Yes, like all kinds of force fields. History has shown us that Warriors and Protectors often pair up to become a stronger force. That's why Daddy asked me if they could see us when we got back to the hotel. You see, there were very powerful wizards at the market today and I could not teleport whilst they had a magical hold on us. Your father hit them hard with his power, releasing us momentarily, which allowed me to move us here. Then I shut them out to stop them from tracking us.'

'I heard Daddy in my head' said Saskia. Everyone looked at her. 'He said, "I'm going to hit them hard, get ready, my darling."'

'Well, what do you know?' said James. 'You heard that?'

'Yes, I often hear your voices in my head. I just thought it was my imagination until now. I heard you scream when Rafi fell, Mummy.' Jenna shot a nervous look at the bedroom where Rafi was asleep. It had been almost forty-eight hours now.

'If you are in tune with humans so closely that you can hear guarded messages *meant for other people*,' James nudged his daughter, smiling, 'then you are more likely to be either a Healer or the last kind and most rare of all wizards,' he paused for dramatic effect, 'an Oracle.'

'What, a fortune teller?' Zachary huffed, clearly not impressed.

'Not just a fortune teller,' James stated sternly. 'Imagine being able to feel what will happen next, being able to block the serpent before it strikes or move a millimetre out the way of an arrow. Knowing what these things will do before they do them is just amazing.'

'Yes, but it's not all about fighting,' Jenna chided, shooting James another look and showing her lack of patience for the constant reference to violence. 'Oracles can see where the goodness in the world can come from and can examine the outcomes of any situation to bend the present for the greater good, as well as being able to see events in the future.'

'What, any event? Like the lottery numbers for next week?' asked Zachary.

'It doesn't work like that, honey,' Jenna giggled. 'Some wizards say that Oracles are in tune with the energy that runs through the universe, giving them an unlimited view of things they are entwined with.'

'What does that mean?' Zachary scrunched his nose up.

'It means it's the most wishy-washy magic you have ever come across, and even the Oracles don't know what they know until it comes to them.' James said this with a ghostly, deep voice and the children giggled. 'The cool stuff is dodging bullets, if you ask me.'

'Spoken like a true Warrior, my love,' Jenna said, shaking her head.

'Who's a Warrior?' came the little tired voice of Rafi, who was now standing in the doorway to the bedroom. He was rubbing his big brown eyes and smiling at the family with his fabulous toothless grin that made him look especially sweet. He was also holding his favourite pink blanket, the one he called 'mau-mau', which made him look even cuter.

'Rafi!' the family yelled and they all leapt up and surrounded the bewildered little boy in a giant hug.

Chapter 6: The Lost City of the Incas

'No, Rafi, you can't have my wand!' said James for the fifth time that morning.

'But I could be a Warrior like you, Daddy!' he repeated for the eighteenth time that hour.

'I know that, sunshine,' James was starting to lose his patience, 'but it's mine and you don't know your element yet.'

'What's an element again?' Rafi asked, padding his little feet behind James into the bathroom.

'Jenna!' James shouted. 'Help me out, honey.'

'Rafi!' called Jenna, who had been listening to her tenacious son driving James up the wall from the excitement that he was now an actual wizard. 'Come here and love your Mummy,' she called. Rafi paused, with indecision in his eyes. He wanted more answers, but they had already repeated everything for him many times. Now Mummy's love was on offer, and this meant everything to the small Mummy's boy. He hesitated, then turned and ran out. James sighed with relief.

The family sat down for a sumptuous breakfast brought to the room by three waiters all dressed in white, who wheeled in three white trollies littered with silver domes that housed the variety of luxury foods James had ordered to cater to all their tastes. James tipped the waiters and showed them out, then smiled to himself as he caught sight of the three children trailing after the smell that now wafted through the suite. They all sat down in the sunshine on the balcony with the city spread out before them.

'Where are we going again?' asked Rafi as the family tucked into the feast before them.

'Machu Picchu.'

'Bless you!' said Zachary, causing the whole family to start giggling.

'It's often referred to as "The Lost City of the Incas".'

'Oooh, now, that does sound cool.'

'It is. Machu Picchu is full of old buildings and tourists. It's even at the top of a mountain.' The children's faces sunk. 'But we are going to the real one—now that should wake you up a bit.'

'The real one?' Rafi looked confused.

'Yes, you will find that most cities, towns, and buildings that are shrouded in historical mystery usually have a link to the world of wizards, like the Lost City of the Incas or the Lost City of Atlantis or Stonehenge, to name a few.' The kids were beaming with excitement. 'We will be going slightly past the tourist version of Machu Picchu to the Urubamba Valley, a hidden city where wizards don't have to hide and all the magical things that surround our world can come out to play and be free. These sites exist for that reason: so we can be free.'

Saskia frowned and James heard her small voice in his head, *'I hope Teivel is not there.'*

'Now, that is just amazing, Saskia.' James directed his comment towards her.

'What is?' Zachary asked.

'I could hear Saskia in my head without trying to. She placed her words in there for me.' He said this last bit as a question and she nodded. 'No, darling, Teivel will not be there. These sites are precious to all wizards everywhere and they are heavily protected from the real world. He wouldn't dare make a move within its walls. There would be too many powerful people to stop him and he could risk exposing the site.'

'What about his friends?' Saskia asked out loud this time.

'Hmm, we didn't cover that bit, did we?' She shook her head. 'A certain little man woke up.' James smiled and leaned over to Rafi and kissed him on his big baby cheeks. 'Jenna, perhaps you could give an impartial view?'

Jenna nodded and began, 'There have been many great and powerful wizards throughout history who have done some wonderful,' she paused, 'and terrible things. Some of these terrible acts have split the wizarding world. Some believe we should be monitored and policed, while others believe we should have our freedom and be left alone. Teivel is part of a corporation that monitors and tries to police all wizarding activities around the world. It is a very large and wealthy group and one that your father and I don't believe in.'

'Who polices the policemen?' James stated firmly.

'Quite! These people are known as "Darwinians" after the famous scientist Charles Darwin. They use scientific knowledge and magic mixed with modern technology, political influence, and great wealth to monitor and manage the wizards around the world.'

'What do they want with us?' Saskia looked afraid.

'They would have seen Rafi's incredible Dawn through their advanced technology, and now, they are looking for him because they are afraid of him. They are now probably looking for you, too.'

'Me! Why me?'

Looking at the angelic little girl with long blonde ringlets in her hair and big blue eyes, James found it hard to believe that anyone would be afraid of her and then he shook himself to his senses. His inner voice knew that they should be scared, and he was.

'Many centuries ago, some great wizards found each other . . .,' Jenna was explaining.

'These were by far the most powerful wizards the world had ever seen,' James interjected and then Jenna continued on.

'They found each other and became a happy family for a while. As time went on, their power and knowledge grew, but they started to argue.' Jenna looked sad. 'They started to torment and hurt the normal people of the world, causing great fear and death through their pettiness, arguments, and great arrogance.' She paused deep in thought. 'The people suffered for many years. Then after a long period of misery, some precious few rose up and started to fight back. Wizards like Daddy.' She looked at him lovingly. 'They bravely fought these cruel wizards, and after many centuries and much loss of life, they destroyed them.' She reached out and grabbed James's hand. 'Those great wizards are known throughout history as the "Gods of Olympus".' The children looked shocked and she let them hang on that for a moment before continuing. 'The Darwinians are scared this will happen again and they will do anything to protect the world from such tyranny.'

'Which is all very noble,' James chided, 'but the kind of power the Gods of Olympus had has not existed for centuries. Now, it is the Darwinians themselves who have grown too strong and powerful. I fear that with their great power, they will become the very thing they fear.' He looked at the children intently. 'That is why I will never join them, ever.'

'It was prophesised many years ago by several great Oracles that the gods would return one day,' Jenna continued. 'This is why they are scared of Rafi and you two.' She placed a gentle hand on the other two children. 'The likes of the explosion and power that came from Rafi's Dawn have not been seen for centuries and could be aligned with him having great power.' She looked at Zachary and Saskia. 'This kind of power is in his blood and has been passed down from generations, which probably means that somewhere in our history, one of our ancestors was one of the gods of Olympus.'

'This also means that you two are highly likely to have the same great power, and that is why they are scared of you, my darling Saskia.' James looked at his daughter with sadness in his eyes. 'We knew mine and Mummy's powers were strong when we met, but we didn't know much about Mummy's family tree. Somewhere in her ancestry, one of her relatives was adopted into a normal family. Imagine their shock when their child Dawned!' He laughed. 'But where this child came from, no one knew. Given that I have traced most of my ancestors, it could be your bloodline that links us back to the gods.' James looked at Jenna. 'Always knew you were trouble,' he said with a chuckle.

'Yeah, it's me that's trouble says the Warrior, ha!'

'So, the Darwinians are scared and will be looking to recruit us all to their great and powerful organisation so that they can control us and gain even greater strength. If indeed you have the power of the gods of Olympus, they will never stop looking for you, and that is a problem.' James frowned. 'However, there are many wizards who have been waiting for their return for centuries and will want to protect, teach, and guide you to becoming leaders of the wizarding world, that is, if you are what they hope you are.'

'These wizards are known as the "League of Olympians" and they represent some of the oldest and most powerful wizards on the planet.'

'Are we part of the League of Olympians, Daddy?' asked Saskia.

'I have never considered myself in the League, though recent events may have changed my mind.' He smiled. 'And I have certainly never been a Darwinian. I have always been a free wizard and tried not to involve myself in the ancient disputes of the various wizarding tribes. There have been many over the centuries: some I have fought for, and others I have turned my back on. The Darwinians are the most powerful tribe I have ever seen, and the first to mix with normal people. They favour using science, technology, and politics to wield power over the free wizards and the League of Olympians alike. I fear them and their rules.

'The League has always been a bunch of old wizards living in the past, preaching of the time when the Darwinians and the rest of the world will have to come to respect the wizarding world. Wizards have had a tough time in history, never quite being able to manage the balance between power and friendship with normal people, and this I understand, having felt the full brunt of how cruel and dangerous people's fear of us is.' He paused and hung his head down.

'What happened, Daddy?' asked Saskia. 'Is that where the marks all over your body came from?'

'Another time, my lovely.' James smiled at her big heart and lay a hand on hers. 'Though I empathise with the League, I cannot approve of either normal people or wizards wielding power over one another, and I would use every last bit of my strength to protect the balance. That is who I am.'

'Who we are,' Jenna said sternly, looking directly at her husband. 'This dispute has been around for centuries and is one we always wanted to stay away from, but we may not have an option now.' She trailed off while looking at her brood.

'That's why we are off to Machu Picchu.'

'Bless you,' said Zachary, causing them all to giggle again. James ruffled his hair.

'Thank you, sunshine. Gwion's newest wife Nellie is an Oracle, and that is who we went to see in the marketplace. Unfortunately, we were in the wrong market. She works at the other one they run, in Machu Picchu.'

'Bless you,' said Rafi.

'And that's where we are off to as soon as you finish your breakfast. Gwion mentioned there is a rodeo happening tonight, so perhaps we will stay the night.' He raised an eyebrow and looked at Jenna, who nodded in agreement.

'Cool!' Zachary piped in.

The family finished their breakfast under the bright sunshine and clear blue skies of Peru, and then made their way into the suite where fresh new clothes were waiting for them, having been purchased by the concierge and carried up with the breakfast. They got dressed amongst the buzz and excitement of the children who were desperate to get to the wizarding city. Once ready, they all assembled in the main lounge wearing big grins and holding hands to form a little circle.

'Daddy . . .' Saskia began.

'Yes?'

'Why does Teivel not like you?' James sighed and smiled down at his daughter.

'Did you see he had a limp?'

'Yes.'

'Well, I gave it to him.'

The family all disappeared in five small swirls of black smoke.

The feeling of teleporting was like a mild version of pins and needles all over your body thought Zachary, but it was over too quickly and his eyes adjusted to the new surroundings. They were in a jungle surrounded by lush green vegetation with the noise of hidden animals everywhere. The children spun round, taking in the unusual scenery and pointing out the glimpses of brightly coloured parrots and unusual plants. It seemed they were walled in on almost all sides by the impenetrable foliage and the children naturally started walking to the only pathway open to them.

They could see through the trees that the jungle seemed to disappear just beyond the area they were in now, and as they got closer the incredible view of the valley before them came into sight. The five tiny specs in the enormous landscape came out onto a ridge looking out over the bright green valley. The steepness of the fall was not un-walkable and the walls of the valley stepped down on giant ledges all the way to the massive base, which spanned out before them and into the distance. The children, upon coming into full view of the valley, stopped immediately and huddled closer to their parents, with all three of them suddenly clinging on out of fear.

'I don't want to go there, Mummy,' Saskia's voice was full of fear.

'Me either,' added the boys.

Jenna crouched down before them and gathered them in her arms.

'Before you is Machu Picchu.'

'Bless you,' said James, trying to lighten the mood, but no one smiled. 'Sorry.'

'This is the Urubamba Valley, the site of the real Lost City, the hidden wizarding city.' Jenna took their little hands

59

and turned them to look out over it and the children huddled in even closer.

'I don't want to go, Mummy. I'm scared. Please, don't make me go,' Saskia pleaded.

'Shh, baby, listen to me carefully. This valley is known as the "Sacred Valley of the Incas".'

'But its original name was the "Scared Valley" because of the feeling you have right now,' said James.

'Quite.' Jenna continued on, shooting him a look. This was her moment to share something. 'Powerful Protectors like me have cast a spell over this valley to make people feel scared as they approach, encouraging them to leave it. They decided that the name "Scared Valley" would only invite thrill seekers and explorers, so over time, it became the . . .'

'. . . Sacred Valley. It's an anagram,' said Zachary, finding it hard to cheer up.

Jenna moved in front of the children again, making sure they could see the valley before them. She squatted to their eye line. She held her hand up high with her palm towards their little faces. Slowly, she moved her hand down, washing the children with her energy, and took in the expressions on their faces as they changed from ones of terror to those of total wonder. After she swept her hand one more time, she let it rest on her lap and turned to see what her and James could see all along, the vibrant buzzing wizarding city of Machu Picchu.

The green hills around the edges were littered with Peruvian-style small grey and brown houses that seemed to fit into their surroundings. All of them sported thatched rooftops with single chimneys. The buildings became denser towards the base of the hills. Where the valley levelled out in the middle, it was tightly packed with larger buildings and the occasional odd-shaped taller structure. Machu Picchu stretched as far as the eye could see, and it reminded Zachary of the city of Cuzco, but hundreds of years older. Smoke plumes signified the presence of working chimneys all over the city and he could make out a large piece of green open land to one side of the valley that led to the dense jungle, which was the only area unencumbered by any buildings.

The city had the aura of magic, and if that was not captivating enough, from their viewpoint, they could see all kinds of skywards activity. To their right, a herd of winged horses were being harnessed above the green open area by what looked like a giant eagle with a small rider. They were doing a terrible job and the horses were splitting up in all directions and then coming back together gracefully into formation. Tiny black dots zoomed up and down and whizzed all around the city. Upon closer inspection, Zachary could make out that these were wizards who were flying all around the buildings and in all directions. Some would burst out high above the rooftops before swooping back down, which caused the children to yelp and point. Larger creatures would fly up momentarily above the structures in various places, and from the distance, it was difficult to make out what they were. James moved over to stand next to Jenna and took her hand.

'I love it here,' he said.

'Me too.'

They both watched as their brood hopped about excitedly, still pointing out the hubbub of activity that was Machu Picchu.

A large shadow overhead made the family turn to look in the opposite direction. They were just in time to see a giant dragon being ridden in by several people just twenty feet overhead, like a jumbo jet coming into land. Instinctively, they all ducked down, though there was plenty of clearance, and they turned to watch the mammoth beast swoop down and make a wavy path towards the large green area, scattering the winged horses to the far reaches of the city before they regrouped overhead again.

'Blimey!' exclaimed Rafi. 'That's a dragon!'

'Yes,' said James, 'many creatures are protected by us from the rest of the world, normally because they were hunted to the point of extinction or because they are naturally very difficult to find, like unicorns for example.'

'Unicorns?' said Zachary.

'Yes, they are the fastest teleporting creatures in the world and are extremely timid, so it's very difficult to see them because they disappear at the slightest noise. Apparently, a herd appeared a few days ago in the forest just beyond where the dragon landed.'

'Cool.'

'Are we going into the city, Mummy?' asked Saskia.

'Yes, darling, but the spell that protects this city shields it from all kinds of senses like sight, sound—even touch— making it very hard to teleport in, so everyone is forced to appear on the outskirts.'

'Which works from a defensive perspective,' said James. 'You can see everyone who is coming in. Good idea, huh?' he smiled.

'Was it your idea, Daddy?' Saskia asked, picking up on his subtlety.

'I may have had a hand in that one in the late 1600s, but I can't take credit for all of it.' He beamed and ruffled her hair. Zachary peered over the ledge they were standing on and turned back to his parents.

'How do we get down from here and into the city?'

James stepped towards him and held out his hands so that Zachary and Saskia took them. Jenna took Rafi's hand and the parents looked at each other.

'Now, that's the fun bit,' said Jenna, before the whole family took off in flight.

Chapter 7: A Magical City

'Whoa!' gasped the children as they hung in the air fifty feet above where they were just standing.

'You ready?' Jenna called out and they all nodded.

The five figures swooped down the green walls of the valley just above the treetops at an incredible speed, zigzagging through branches that stuck out above the canopy until they reached the edge of the city, when James, Zachary, and Saskia split out from the other two and went in an arc that took them extremely high, spiralling in circles as they climbed.

'Flying!' James called out to the two children in his grip. 'That is something Warriors do really well!' And the three figures stalled in the air for a second and then plummeted down at a mind-blowing speed to join Jenna and Rafi again.

'Whoooaaa!' called the two children again.

'I think I left my lunch up there!' Zachary called out through a massive smile.

'Me too!' yelled Saskia.

The five figures darted all around the city and the children took in all the odd sights and funny-looking buildings until they eventually came swooping down for a landing on the edge of the green opening where the dragon had landed. All eyes were now on the giant green beast that was lying down some way into the plain.

'So, you decided to take us to the giant fire-breathing, man-eating dragon over there?' Saskia asked.

'Ha! Actually, most dragons are placid, quiet herbivores,' James responded. 'The fire-breathing, man-eating kind are incredibly rare now, because they have been hunted down through fear to the point of extinction.'

'Oh, really?'

'Yes. You obviously have to be careful of their size, but most dragons have similar habits and temperaments to elephants. Having faced some of the fire-breathing kind, I am rather fond of the herbivore variety. Anyway, it's not her we are here to see, but this: the famous wizarding market of Ziwardine.'

The children cast their eyes away from the dragon and into the stalls, tents, and gatherings of people before them. Like the market of San Pedro in Cuzco, it was full of wonder and bright colours, except this market had people and creatures flying in and out from all angles.

'We are here to visit Gwion's other stall, where his wife, Nellie, is waiting for us. Nellie is a famous and rare Oracle and I believe it is within her power to put the notion that you three are the second coming out the window once and for all, giving us some peace and quiet to get back to our lives.'

'Or not,' said Jenna.

'That's the positive spirit, darling,' James said sarcastically.

The family made their way into the throng of the marketplace and took in all of its wondrous sights.

It was a hot day. The close quarters of the market and all the buyers made it stifling. They moved in slow procession as the way ahead offered only a single channel that occasionally broke into some dead-end paths that housed smaller, less popular stalls. The market was only wide enough to fit four people standing side by side in some parts, but there was nothing consistent about it. Overhead, there was a mix of canopies, sheets, and corrugated steel, all supported and held in place in different ways and overlaying each other to form a single covering that led the whole way through the single channel. The path led slightly uphill through the marketplace. As they walked up, the merchants called out all kinds of sales pitches to the passers-by.

'Try this!'

'Come here! Look, look, best in the world.'

'Pretty lady, come closer!'

'Handsome boy, look at this.'

The merchants were very loud and brash and would call to each other occasionally in a language unfamiliar to the children, seemingly sharing private jokes most likely at the punter's expense. At such moments, they shared a laugh before quickly continuing their calls. This marketplace had less manners than the San Pedro one, but it was far more exciting and lively. The stalls seemed to be grouped by produce, and so far, the family had been strolling slowly past powders of all different sizes. They were shaped like termite mounds of the brightest colours nature had to offer. There was every colour imaginable, from bright greens to pinks that would definitely glow in the dark, and the merchants were pointing to the different mounds and calling out facts about them. A squat man with a big grin waved a dark blue powder in the palm of his hand under Jenna's nose.

'Increase your powers by over one hundred times with one spoonful in your coffee!'

'No thank you.' Jenna moved her head away and held the children close.

'Mummy,' Saskia whispered, 'maybe you should buy some.'

'Yes, yes, you buy.' The seller sensed a sale upon hearing Saskia's whisper. 'Listen to the girl.'

'No, no, but thank you.' Jenna shuffled past faster, pushing the people ahead and the seller called out something that made his colleague laugh as another punter came up and they started to haggle aggressively.

'Please, don't encourage them darling. Most of these things are "fizz-bangs".' Saskia looked confused and Jenna continued, 'like a small firework, they will be impressive only long enough for a "fizz and a bang," and then they are done—good for small thrills only.' Saskia nodded and a booming deep voice made her look up.

'You, sir, change your wizarding type from Warrior to Oracle with this new potion,' an obese man with a large black beard and a bald head called out, looking at James.

'How did he know Daddy was a Warrior?' Saskia whispered too loudly again, and the big man's face broke into a large toothy grin and he continued on. 'Because I have used this switching potion to make me an Oracle, so I can tell what wizards you all are.' He waved his hands at an eight foot high bright yellow powder pile near him. 'Rub four fistfuls on your palms per day and you will be able to see the future.'

James turned and looked at Jenna with an eyebrow raised. She heard his voice in her head.

'Maybe we could try it and find out what the kids are without Nellie.'

'It's utter rubbish and you know it—what a waste of time and money!'

'We have plenty of money.'

'And if you think you have discovered what the children are from this merchant, then what?'

'I will want to find Nellie to tell us anyway, because I won't trust it.' James's face dropped.

'Exactly.'

'But you can trust it. We only sell the best in Sabashi's stall!' came the loud voice of the merchant. James, Jenna and Saskia, who had been listening in on the conversation, all turned to look at him. 'We also sell listening powder.' He smiled and raised his closed fist high and ran a silver powder to his other hand. He winked at the couple.

'No thanks, Sabashi,' James said curtly and frowned deeply.

Sabashi knew people well, and he understood that he had pushed too hard. He backed off, bowing gently, and called out to the next group of passers-by: 'Change your wizarding type!'

'Mummy, I'm too hot!' called out Rafi, whilst being pushed around by the crowds.

'Me too!' chorused the other children.

'Blimey! It is a bit close today darling,' James said.

'I think I see something that will help just ahead.' Jenna pointed to a huddle of people around a merchant who was fervently working to serve all the visitors. The family pushed their way through, and much to their relief, the market channel grew into an open-air section that was three times wider than the path they had come from. A few people grumbled and took flight as soon as the canopy offered the opening, while others streamed in and headed immediately for the crowd that the family now approached.

'Cooling potion! Cheapest in the market—lasts all day,' called out the merchant.

The children brightened upon hearing this and James pushed his way through. A few buyers shouted at him and he turned, looking ferociously at them. They backed off, some nodding at him as if greeting an acquaintance, and he continued towards a very tall muscly man at the front who was being served.

The tall man must have been at least nine feet high and the merchant needed a step ladder to pour the powder over his head. Immediately, a light opaque blue film spread out over his skin and faded into invisibility.

'Ahh,' called out the man in a deep voice, 'that's better,' and he turned awkwardly to leave the throng. As he did so, he locked eyes with James. A look of surprise washed over his face and they both stared at each other for a second. James's family watched them in the midst of the crowd and tensed up. The large man rested his big hand on James's shoulder and smiled without saying a word. His smile was a warm one, and then he quite abruptly nodded and continued on his path. James paused and then pushed on to the front.

As the large man broke free of the crowd, the children gasped at his appearance. He was a man for the top half of his body and from the waist down he was a large muscly horse. He heard their reaction and turned to face Jenna and the three children, whose mouths hung open. He knelt down on one of his front legs to form a gracious and slow bow before standing back at full height, pushing his chest out, holding his head high, and marching off.

'He's a centaur,' Jenna whispered as the children faced her, still with their mouths open. 'Perhaps I should have given you some warning, but this market is full of magical people and creatures, so be prepared for a few more shocks.'

'It's not full of them. We've only seen one so far,' protested Zachary.

'Really? Look closer.'

The children looked around for a few seconds and turned back to Jenna.

'Where?' asked Zachary in a moody voice.

Jenna rolled her eyes at Saskia.

'*Boys can never see anything,*' she spoke in her head and Saskia giggled.

'What?' Zachary piped up again.

'Look at the crowd. What do you see?'

The children looked back at the pushing throng of hot people and watched the relief of the customers being served. Finally, they noticed that there were other oddities about the scene before them. One smaller man had hoofs for feet and Jenna pointed him out as being a faun, half human and half goat. He was accompanied by two others like him. A very large woman was wrestling with something under her blouse that occasionally leapt up to block her face. Each time the incident occurred, she would push down violently, cursing at the hidden creature. There was a round smiley man leaving the crowd after having just been cooled with a tiny version of himself sitting on his shoulder also smiling.

The children pointed and whispered to each other and Jenna scolded them gently for pointing. Then she came in close and told them to watch a man and woman who were holding hands and heading towards them from the cooling stall. They both had long, thick blond hair, bright searing blue eyes, and pale skin that seemed to glow, and they stood about six feet tall with athletic bodies. They were wearing matching white togas and sandals, and they both carried white sacks on their backs. The man turned to face his partner, took her other hand, and smiled at her. She returned his smile and they peacefully leaned in and kissed each other. With a shrug of their shoulders, they released their white sacks, which fell down beside their waists, revealing large white-feathered wings that they stretched out as if waking them from a sleep.

The passers-by all stopped and watched, some having to move out of the way of the thick, powerful wings. The couple began to flap them slowly at first and then they twitched to life with some unnatural fast movements. They pulled their wings back in and crouched down, still holding hands. Their eyes were locked onto each other's, and in a flash, they leapt beyond the market canopy. Everyone left on the ground craned their necks up to watch them hit a peak at about twenty-five feet before they spread their wings out fully to take flight, and then they were gone. An eerie silence filled the market, which had come to a halt to watch the spectacle, but a single call from the cooling stand merchant burst the bubble, and the throng came back to life again.

'Were they angels?' asked Zachary.

'Everyone thinks that when they first see Seraphites.' Jenna smiled. 'They are named after "Seraphs", a word that means "angels", but whilst they are placid people who rarely mix with anyone else, they are known for having terrible, uncontrollable rages if you anger them. They also happen to have one of the strongest armies the world has ever known. Your father might be able to tell you more about them.'

On cue, James arrived with five small sacks in his hand.

'Blimey! I have been in some battles in my life, but that one was worse than fighting pixies.' He opened the first bag and placed it over Saskia. 'Ladies first,' he said and poured the grains over her head. A light-blue film spread out over her pale sweaty skin and her expression changed immediately to that of wonder. She looked up with her big blue eyes and smiled at her parents. Next, James went to pour one over Jenna, who insisted the children go first. Rafi and Zachary followed Saskia with equal wonder, and then the whole family was cool at last. They set off past the cooling stand and went deeper into the market.

The stalls changed from having colourful powders to colourful foods and the sellers continued to call out their wares.

'Mood food, mood food! Be happy, be sad. Be in love or make someone love you!' the hidden voice called out.

'Health food! Be healthy and slim overnight! Lose weight in minutes! Make someone sick!' came another voice, and the children marvelled at the possibilities that sprang to mind. They continued their journey, ignoring the food merchants until one called out something the parents knew would entice their children beyond anything else they had seen.

'Sweets, deserts, ice cream of all kinds! Come and make your sweet tooth happy.'

The children eyed the boundless jars full of assorted shapes and bright colours with a longing, and then turned their gazes to their parents.

'Oh, go on then.' Jenna caved in. 'Only one each,' she added.

'One!' Zachary exclaimed.

'One is more than enough,' James pitched in, 'and we are in a hurry.'

The merchant welcomed the children with the enthusiasm of a guaranteed sale.

'Come, come, what can I get you lovely children?'

'Have you got any chews?' asked Zachary.

'Chews from all over the world!' he cried out loudly enough for other passers-by to hear. 'I have never-ending chews, chews that change colour, chews that will give you a rash,' he whispered, 'to get out of school,' and winked, 'or chews to make you invisible.'

'How about just plain old tasty chews?' Zachary interrupted, and the merchant looked shocked.

'Plain old chews, eh? Hmm . . .' He thought for a second and then smiled. 'How about these?' He picked up a large glass jar full of different coloured balls no bigger than a marble.

'These are Rechewvinators!' He presented the jar with the lid off, so that Zachary got a good look inside.

'Rechewvinators,' repeated Zachary.

'Yes, you enjoy them for at least ten minutes and then remove them from your mouth and let them dry out and they rejuvenate back to the same size and flavour, ready for another chew.' He smiled.

'Brilliant! Have you got a strawberry flavour?'

'Of course,' the merchant smiled, and he handed Zachary a red ball that he popped into his mouth immediately and started chewing with a big smile. 'Who is next? Perhaps this little Seraphite?' he asked and looked at Saskia.

'Do you have any bubble-gum?'

'Oh, only the best bubble-gum in the universe!' He turned and placed the jar with the Rechewvinators back and moved over to a giant green glass vase filled to the brim with what looked like coloured popcorn pieces and took one out. 'This is trouble-double gum.' The merchant beamed. 'It lasts twice as long as normal gum and allows the chewer to blow bubbles double the size of normal gum.'

'That sounds great! But where is the "trouble" in that?'

'Because once chewed, it can stick anything together permanently, so be careful where you throw it away.'

'Okay. I'll take that please.' Saskia put out her hand.

'And finally the young master.' The merchant looked at Rafi.

'Do you have anything chocolaty?' Rafi asked in a shy quiet voice.

'Only the finest chocolate on this side of the planet.' He puffed up his chest and spun round, scurrying into his stall. The merchant came back a moment later with a silver goblet full of brown drop-shaped chocolate pieces. 'These are chocolate pops.' He lowered the goblet to show Rafi the chocolate pieces inside and his eyes lit up.

'Don't you mean chocolate drops?'

'No, I mean chocolate pops.'

'What do they do?' Rafi asked.

'They taste like chocolate,' the merchant said and let out a big laugh. Then he leaned in close to Rafi and whispered, 'And they make you fart louder than an elephant.' He straightened himself and winked.

'Yes, please!' Rafi giggled and held his hand out.

The merchant put five pops into a little bag and gave them to Rafi. James walked over and settled the bill and the family were off down the market channel once again. The food stalls turned into displays of books and ancient artefacts, and it was now Jenna's turn to be lured into the stalls. She picked up ancient books and classic wands, asking the sellers questions about each one. They were making painfully slow progress and James was gradually losing his patience.

Jenna was holding a book titled, *A History of Ancient Demon Warriors* when a voice in the next stall made her look up.

'Special elements! Extremely rare fire dragon skin, griffin fur, fairy hair!' the merchant called.

Jenna frowned, put the book down, and hurried the family on past the stall with urgency. As they passed the stall owner, James looked him over and noticed he was classically creepy enough to be selling such horrid items. He was tall, dark, and thin, with long straggly greasy hair and an unkempt beard to match. His eyes were deep set and black and his skin was pale. The merchant had a long, crooked nose and a sullen face. If there was ever a man whose appearance alone made him evil, it was him.

The man stared back at James and without saying a word, a dark voice sounded in his head.

'What do you need? Tell me what you require and I'll get it—no questions asked.'

James shook his head to clear his thinking and ignored the voice.

The market opened out a little and the sound and smell of livestock came floating down the channel. It was like some sort of zoo without any health and safety considerations, as there seemed too little in the way of barriers from the creatures being sold. This was ok for the first few stands, which had no room for large animals, but the roars and sounds that came from up ahead were enough to set the mind spinning with anxiety. The children huddled closer to their parents as they walked along, and Zachary couldn't help but feel sorry for the animals being lined up, discussed, and sold.

'What you lookin at!' came the angry snap from a faun selling chickens who had noticed Rafi staring at him.

'I'm so sorry. He has never seen a faun up close before and he's still so little,' said Jenna.

'Well, teach him some manners. Rude little child!' snapped the faun.

'Perhaps you would like a lesson in manners?' chided James, stepping into view. He had lagged behind a little to look at some pigs with Saskia.

'So-so-sorry, old master,' the faun stuttered and bent into a low bow.

'Have some care for a lady and her child!' snapped James.

'Yes. Of course, old master—so sorry sir.'

'Let's go.' James herded the family on.

'Friend of yours?' whispered Jenna. 'He seems nice,' she said with a smirk.

'No friend of mine darling. Fauns have an excellent sense of danger, probably from their goat genes, and he read me like a book and knew he was in peril.' He whispered the next sentence in her ear. 'They generally have no pride and will beg, plead, or tell you anything if they are afraid. That's worth remembering.'

The children were suddenly running around, hooting and pointing excitedly at the large stalls which housed bears, giraffes with their heads sticking above the canopy, tigers, horses, and all kinds of insects and snakes. James grabbed the back of Rafi's clothes to keep him from sticking his hand through a wooden barrier where two tigers were quickly approaching. As they came close to the edge, an invisible force field shocked them into retreating.

James was distracted from telling him off by Saskia tugging on their clothes.

'Look, look!' Saskia cried excitedly and pointed to where the boys were huddled around a plump woman wearing an old-fashioned milkmaid's dress, complete with a white apron. She was sitting on a small wooden stool and feeding a litter of baby dragons with an oversized baby bottle.

'Come on you lot,' James called and he herded the reluctant children past the next few stands until more distractions were upon them in the form of food, complete with jugglers, acrobats, and musicians to entertain and glean money from the hungry punters. James purchased three hot dogs and handed one each to the children, as they watched a juggler who was floating a multitude of balls in a synchronised aerial performance. The enjoyment lasted until Jenna noticed a small grubby boy of about eleven slip his hand into Zachary's side pocket, where he had put the rechewvinators. She turned to the would-be pickpocket and projected her voice into his head.

'*Don't you dare!*' she snapped silently.

The boy jumped back and looked for the source of the voice. He found Jenna's stare, to which he smiled, curtseyed, and ran off.

'Let's go!' she called.

'Oh, I wanted to see the finale,' said James. 'He was gonna do it on an eleven-foot unicycle.' Then he sensed Jenna's disquiet. 'What's the matter?'

'Nothing. Let's find Nellie. There are too many distractions here that are keeping us from what is important.'

They moved on to the next set of stalls, which were selling weapons and armour. Now, it was James's turn to be distracted. He was preoccupied until Rafi picked up an axe that swung itself and embedded its head deep into a wooden post holding up part of the market canopy. The owner came rushing out.

'I'm so sorry!' he called 'Is he ok? I should have been watching.'

He was a very dark and handsome man with incredible muscles all over, a soft face with chiselled features and piercing blue eyes.

'No, I should have been watching him,' Jenna responded without looking whilst struggling to remove the axe from the post.

'Blimey, strong little fella, isn't he?'

Jenna turned and gawped at the stunning muscle-bound merchant, who reached out with one hand and removed the axe as if it were embedded in butter.

'Er, yes, erm, I guess so . . .' was all she could manage.

'Mark Anthony, at your service. See anything you like?' Flirting came naturally to Mark.

'Yes—er, I mean, no. Thank you though.' Jenna became flustered

'Perhaps there's something I can help you with. We sell all kinds of weapons to help damsels in distress.' He casually blocked her path to prevent her and Rafi from leaving the area.

'She won't be in distress as long as I am around,' came James's voice from behind Mark, and he spun round at an incredible speed while James swung a strong and fast punch directly at his head. Mark ducked it with ease and swung back. James caught the fist in mid-flight, awakening Mark's reflexes and rage at the shock of someone being able to catch his punch in such a manner. He wore the shock all over his face and James stood before him, grinning.

'I don't believe it! Is it really you? Stone me, James, it's been over a hundred years.'

'Hello Mark, it's great to see you. This is Jenna, my wife.'

'We've met,' said Jenna.

'Yes, sorry about that. If I'd have known . . . .' He gestured between Jenna and James and she blushed.

'Ha! I wouldn't expect a few hundred years to change you, old friend.' He turned to his children. 'Kids, this is Mark Anthony, another really old friend of mine. This is Zachary, Saskia, and Rafi.' He pointed to each one of the children and they all shook his hand. James leaned into the kids and told them in a staged whisper, 'he's even older than me.'

'Yeah, yeah, less of the "old", matey.'

'Ha! Mark was a centurion in the Roman army.'

'I think I have heard of you and Cleopatra in our history lessons,' said Saskia.

'Close, but I came a few generations after that Mark Anthony. I am a direct descendant of his.' Mark puffed out his chest. 'I was named after him.'

'Yeah, right, and I'm a direct descendent of Dolly Parton,' said James, and everyone, including Mark, started laughing.

'You're closer to Hades, you little devil.'

James mouthed to him to be quiet at this statement and tilted his head towards the children. Mark mouthed back a 'sorry', but Saskia saw the exchange and made a mental note to ask about it later.

'Does Gwi know you are here?' asked Mark.

'Yeah, I saw him yesterday in San Pedro Market and we were, well, erm, "interrupted", shall we say.'

'I heard there was trouble with some irritants from the organisation. That was you, wasn't it?'

'Unfortunately, it was, but it is Nellie we are here to see.'

Mark raised his head in curiosity.

'Really, what's up?'

'Nothing much, I just have a few questions about this little fella,' he said and picked up Rafi. James blew a raspberry on Rafi's cheek and the little boy giggled. Mark held James and Jenna's gazes for a few seconds and nodded.

'*He must have heard the rumours about Rafi. He knows why we are here. Tell him. He could help us,*' came the voice of Jenna in James's head.

'*He is and always will be an ally. Just leave it until we know the truth,*' James responded.

'You know it's rude to whisper,' said Mark, who had noticed the silence and realised that they were talking in their heads. Jenna blushed and James laughed.

'Sorry, still sharp then?'

'Not bad for an old man, eh?' said Mark. 'Come. Gwion's a bit further down. I'll walk you there. Are you sticking around? You know there's a rodeo on tonight—should be good, and I heard a rumour that Skinny is in town.'

'Blimey, Skinny! I'd love to catch up with him too.'

The family walked down the market listening to James and Mark chatting animatedly and laughing about old friends and times. With these two big men guiding them along, the mood was jovial. Mark asked questions and laughed with the kids. He was naturally very likeable, and had a twinkle in his eye that people warmed to. The stalls were starting to sell household goods, including furniture, and Jenna knew that they were close. Mark was telling the children a funny story about James falling head first into a giant muddy puddle, making them all laugh, when they heard a sudden excited chirping. Mark looked up in shock.

'Quickly, we need to move past this stand.' He cast a sharp look at James.

'Come kids. Let's go quickly.'

The stand was completely covered with black leather boxes of all sizes, but generally they were small, the size of a lunch box. As the family approached, the boxes started to make squeaks and chirps that got louder and louder as they got closer. When James stepped closer to guide Rafi on, his close proximity triggered a more violent response, and the boxes started to vibrate in addition to the squeaking and chirping as if going into overdrive.

'Come on, quickly now!' James shouted above the noise, hustling the family on. Jenna, James, and Mark looked around with concerned expressions on their faces as all eyes were on them. As they left the stand behind, the vibrating slowed down and the noises started to fade.

Suddenly, a loud squeaky voice with an Irish accent called out, 'Beware, the devils are amongst us! My pixies can sense your evil.'

A small old man, no taller than four feet, leapt up with incredible agility onto one of the larger boxes. He was wearing a very smart grey three-piece suit and had a matching top hat. His face was thin with pointy features and he had long, thick sideburns that crept down to his jaw. The small man stood with his legs astride and hands on his hips at first. Then he raised his right hand and pointed it at James and Mark.

'Damn you back to the depths of the Earth, you evil monsters!' he shouted.

James and Jenna continued to hurry the children along, but as he finished the last sentence, Mark paused, looked at James, and smiled.

'Back in a sec,' he said and winked.

'Mark, don't. He's just an angry leprechaun. You know what they are like, always shouting at someone.'

'Yeah, but someone's got to teach this one some manners.'

Mark approached the stall and the leather boxes went into overdrive again. The leprechaun seemed to shrink back as he approached.

'Away with you, devil! It will take me all night to calm down my pixies from fear of your evil. Away with you!' he shouted, but with less venom than before.

A long scaly bright red tail suddenly slithered out the back of Mark's trousers and whipped around in the air with a violent swish. The leprechaun jumped high, away from Mark, but the tail caught him with incredible speed and wrapped around him tight, holding his arms clamped against his body in its grip. Mark's tail carried the leprechaun over the boxes and held him at head height just ahead of where he stood.

'Devil, devil! Help me, help me! Beware a devil!' the leprechaun screamed.

'Silence!' Mark bellowed in a booming voice that echoed through the market. His tail tightened around the tiny man and a small red triangular tip flattened over the leprechaun's mouth, making him now completely terrified and pale.

'I said SILENCE!' he bellowed again, and this time, his skin turned bright red. The whites of his eyes blackened and he looked terrifying. The leprechaun's own eyes seemed to be screaming.

At this moment, the boxes went completely silent and still, matching the rest of the market. It was eerily quiet and Mark brought the leprechaun close to his face.

'Now, how do you teach a leprechaun manners?' he hissed in a deep low voice.

'Leave him, Mark.' James had walked up behind him and placed a hand on his shoulder.

'Why should I? What have I done to him?' he hissed at the small man without turning to look at James.

'Nothing, but this is not how to teach him. Rise above his ignorance and show him you are better than he is,' he said in a calm voice.

A long pause followed and then Mark screwed up his face.

'Aaah,' he hissed into the face of the terrified leprechaun. Then his tail threw him back across to the boxes where he flipped over in mid-flight to land squarely on his feet facing Mark.

'Away with you, small man with a small mind,' said Mark as his colour and voice came back to normal and his tail whipped back into his clothes. The little man placed his hands back on his hips and stuck his tongue out. He wiggled it around before quickly leaping off the boxes and disappearing into the depths of his stall.

Slowly, the noise of the market returned as everyone realised the spectacle was over. Mark and James joined the rest of the family further up the market in silence.

'Aaawkward,' came the little voice of Saskia breaking the silence, and Jenna smiled.

Three little pairs of eyes stared at Mark and he looked back at the three children, realising they knew nothing about what they had just seen.

'Have I just caused you an issue?' he muttered in the direction of Jenna and James.

'There are a few conversations we haven't had yet, and that was one of them,' said Jenna.

'Oh no! Sorry.' He looked at the kids and half smiled awkwardly.

'It's ok. We need to tell them. It's just that they have taken in a lot over the last few days.'

'I'm sure, but I am sorry anyway.'

'Daddy?' whispered Rafi.

'Yes, little man?'

'What was that?' He pointed a little finger at Mark. Both Zachary and Saskia were closing in on them to listen.

'Ah, that is a conversation we will have tonight.'

'But Dad, he has a tail,' said Rafi too loudly, and Mark shot a 'sorry' look at James.

'I know—well, not quite—but later, later, I promise.'

'Here we are,' Mark called out in hopes of distracting the children from their current conversation. 'Afternoon Gwi! Look who I found.' He placed a hand on the shoulder of what could only have been Gwion from behind.

The family all approached. They were interrupting Gwion, who had been talking to Grub and Patrick. All of three were facing away from the group. Gwion was pointing at their stock and giving the boys instructions about where to display items. He finished his sentence and the boys listened before all three turned around. It was at this moment that James and Jenna realised they had forgotten to have another conversation with their children.

The three massive men turned to greet their visitors with a warm welcome and were wearing big smiles, but whilst they were the same in every way from the day before, there was one major difference in both Gwion and Patrick: they both had one giant eye in the middle of their faces where two should have been.

'Aaahhh!' screamed the kids as they shrunk away behind their parents.

James and Jenna looked shocked and embarrassed at the same time.

'So sorry Gwi. Kids, it's ok. They are a family of Cyclopes— we forgot to mention it. I'm sorry kids, and so sorry Gwi.' Pleaded James.

Slowly, calm spread through the children again and Zachary started giggling.

'Blimey Dad, a little warning would have been good.'

'Yeah Dad, crikey!' Saskia pitched in.

Rafi was still snuggled in tight behind Jenna's leg.

'Hi Gwi,' Zachary spoke to the giant feeling braver now. 'How come you had two eyes last time?'

The big man smiled, his toothy grin and kind face were infectious enough to make the children feel at ease.

'Well, I guess you could call it a little disguise through a small manifestation. Don't you think I would draw a tiny bit of attention if people could see what I really look like?'

'I guess so.'

'All Cyclopes have to use a little magic in this way to be able to go out into the non-magical world. Otherwise, we would be targeted and singled out or even hunted.'

'Really, why?' said Saskia. 'I like your eye.'

Gwion laughed a deep belly laugh.

'That's very nice of you Sassy, can I call you that?'

She nodded.

'But think about how mankind singles out their own kind for being different by things such as the colour of their skin or nationality or even the fact that they like a different football team. Now imagine how the world would react if they knew Cyclopes were living amongst them.'

'So, you're like us then. We have to keep quiet about being wizards for the same reason.'

'You are a very smart young lady,' he said, producing three lollipops from his pocket. 'And here is your reward for being so smart and pretty.'

He handed her a lolly and gave one each to the two boys.

'To the next generation of Warriors.' Gwion smiled at the two boys.

'Why has Grub got two eyes?' asked Rafi.

'Ah, the runt of the litter.' He nudged his son affectionately. 'Takes after his mother—that's why we gave him a good solid Cyclopean name, to remind him of his roots.'

'Speaking of which . . . .' said James.

'Did somebody say witch!' came the strong woman's voice from behind where they were standing.

Nellie stood just beyond the group in the middle of the market channel with her fists clenched on her hips and legs apart, forming an image of strength. She was of an average height, with a curvy figure, thick curly red hair, and high cheek bones that revealed dimples when she smiled. Her green eyes were flecked with twinkles as she took in the sight of the family before her.

'Nellie!' James called out and moved in to throw his arms around her.

Nellie hugged him back and the two embraced for a moment. Then she broke away and clipped him on the head.

'What was that for!' said James jovially.

'Where have you been all this time young man? Not a single call or note.' She chided him.

James looked embarrassed.

'I have been busy, sorry Nell.'

'I can see.' She stretched out her hand towards Jenna. 'Nellie Herakleios, it's lovely to meet you.'

'Lovely to meet you too, Nellie.' Jenna beamed.

'Gwi said you were beautiful, and for once he didn't exaggerate.'

Jenna blushed

'Thank you,' she muttered.

'And who are these lovely children?'

'This is Zachary, Saskia, and Rafael.' Jenna pointed out each child, and in turn they stepped forward and shook Nellie's hand.

'Well, how delightful!'

'Nellie, we need your help.'

'I knew you were coming. I dreamt about it two weeks ago. Didn't I, Gwi? You came to me for help and then blew up most of the city.' She laughed, but James frowned.

'Was it a real dream? Is that going to happen?'

'Not sure. Couldn't tell, but I hope not.' Nellie smiled through an anxious look. 'Why don't we head back to our place and then we can take a closer look, shall we? I expect there is a particular question on your lips.'

'That would be great Nell, thanks.'

'Now that you have been through the market, perhaps we should go the quick route home. Ever been flying with your Dad, kids?'

'First time ever today!' Zachary answered excitedly.

'He's fast isn't he? And a real show-off.' Nellie giggled at her own joke. 'Gwion, be a love and make an exit for us, would you?'

The big man stretched a hand up and pulled on the canopy in a selected area that he knew was detachable, and then he created a person-size hole. The sun beamed in and brought along the midday heat just as the family started to feel the effects of the cooling potion wearing off. Nellie gave a knowing look to Jenna and James, then produced a small leather pouch from her pocket and poured some of the contents into her hand.

'It's hot today, eh?' she said and sprinkled more cooling potion on everyone.

'She knew,' Saskia whispered to Jenna.

Nellie couldn't hear the words, but knew what was being said.

'Let's go.' Nellie beckoned as she levitated upwards towards the gap. 'Oh, watch your trousers going through the hole, Zachary.' With that, she darted through. Jenna took Rafi and Saskia's hands and the three of them took off.

'Whoa! I love flying,' said Saskia.

The three of them zoomed through the opening in single file, with Jenna guiding the children with hand gestures. Next, James and Zachary levitated.

'See you later, at the rodeo?' Mark asked James.

'Me and the boys are camping out to get a good spot—you're both welcome to join us, and your family, James.' Gwion directed his offer towards the two men.

'Definitely, sounds great. See you later then!' James said, excited to spend some time with his old friends.

James and Zachary then darted through the hole.

'Aaaaah!' called out Zachary. He had caught his trousers on a jagged edge of the canopy and it had cut his leg.

'Let me see.'

James flew down and looked through the tear.

'Just a tiny scratch. You'll live.'

He flew up and ruffled Zachary's hair.

'How did she know?' asked Zachary.

'She's an Oracle. She hears and knows a lot more than she lets on. If I think about it, it makes me feel uncomfortable around her, so I try not to. Come on.'

They zoomed upwards to join the others in a big circle in the sky.

'Right, we're all here then. You ok?' Nellie directed towards Zachary.

'Yeah, I should have listened. Sorry.'

'Well, what will really boggle you later is thinking about how would you have stopped it from happening even if you had?' She raised an eyebrow at this question. 'Right, follow me everyone!'

Nellie flew off in the direction of the surrounding hills and headed towards a group of white huts.

Chapter 8: The Prophecy

They landed in the thick vegetation of the surrounding green hills, which had been cut back to form an opening and sculpted to imitate the look of a lush English garden, complete with a white picket fence that gave way to the jungle just beyond it. It was a welcome sight of home with a little white cottage sitting in the centre of the plot. Its roof was thatched, its walls were cobbled, and its windows were leaded. This house would have best been placed in the English countryside, and not the jungles of South America.

'Gorgeous cottage,' said Jenna.

'Thank you. It's taken a few years to get it to look this way, but it reminds me of home. Gwi's a pretty good gardener.' She gestured to the perfect little country garden.

'He is. Perhaps he could come and do mine.' Then Jenna remembered she no longer had a home and felt upset. Nellie came over and put a hand on her arm, squeezing gently.

'Let's go inside and have a cup of tea, shall we?'

Jenna nodded and they entered.

The house was as pretty and delicate inside as it was outside. It hardly seemed like it could have been the home of three large men. The only noticeable features indicating that Gwion and the boys lived here were the very tall doorways and high ceilings. The group made their way through the hallway that was littered with ornaments and antiques. As Jenna passed a large antique display cabinet, she was surprised to see hundreds of tiny little statues of little pink pigs posed as if they were performing all sorts of activities. There were pigs surfing, playing tennis, painting, and writing. There were even groups modelled together as if they were interacting: one pig watched another pig break dancing, while in another group, one drove a car and others waved at the driver.

The kitchen was spacious and kept the country theme with its wooden matching cabinets and a big white butler sink. The room was open plan and was connected to a conservatory with a large round wooden table. A large metal bowl full of twigs sat in the centre of the table and it was surrounded by ten large chairs. The glass room made the most of their beautiful surroundings and Jenna wandered into it in awe.

'This room is amazing! What a view.'

'It's my favourite room of the house,' Nellie said proudly.

Jenna noticed more little pig statues on the kitchen window shelf and even more on the conservatory's window ledges.

'I see you have more friends in here, too.' Jenna pointed to the little statues.

'Yes, I felt how you noticed my little habit in the hallway.' She smiled. 'I have collected pigs since I was a little girl and never stopped. It's silly really.'

'No, I like them.'

'No you don't,' said Nellie, 'but you do find it sweet that I collect them.'

Jenna blushed at her stupidity with being caught out by someone who could feel her thoughts.

'Don't worry, my love.' Nellie continued on, seeing Jenna blush, 'No one likes them, but for some reason, they make me happy—until Gwi turns up with one for dinner.' She grimaced. 'Right, let's get some tea going.'

She put cold water into several cups with a tea bag and then waved her hand over them and passed the piping hot tea to Jenna and James.

'It's much better than a kettle, eh?' she said, addressing the children after having felt their excitement at the small bit of magic. They all nodded.

'Have a seat. I'll prepare for a reading.'

Nellie raised her right hand and then threw it out towards the metal bowl on the table, as if throwing an imaginary object. Immediately, the bowl flashed and then crackled as a small fire rose out of it.

She then waved two fingers towards the slanted windows at the top of the room and they opened, allowing the smoke out. Next, she pointed the same two fingers at the neatly rolled up curtains at the top of each window and they rolled down gently, blocking out all the light except for the small windows at the top that were letting out the smoke. The room was now dim and the small flames from the fire danced around, making magical shadows everywhere.

'There, that's better. Everyone sit please.'

Everyone took up a chair at the large round table.

'Now, what would you like to discuss?' She looked at Jenna and James.

'You know why we are here Nellie,' James answered.

'Yes, but it's polite to ask.' She smirked. 'I know that you want to know your element.'

She directed at Zachary and he nodded. She took his hand and reached out, dipping her hand in the naked flames of the small fire in front of her. She scooped up some ash from the base of the bowl.

'My element is ash and I have found fresh warm ash seems to work best.'

Nellie held her hand out, palm up, and closed her fingers around the ash tightly, shutting her eyes. She opened them again almost immediately with a look of shock.

'The Crack of Dawn has not arrived for this child yet.'

'That's right,' Jenna said, now looking very anxious.

'This will limit what I can tell you about him—including your element, my lovely.' She directed the latter part of her comment towards Zachary. 'You see, until you are a fully awakened wizard, your body may not even know the answer to that question and many more, I'm afraid. One thing I can tell you is that an explosion is coming of incredible size and this resembles his Dawn. Jenna, you need to be ready.'

She nodded, but tears were welling up in her eyes.

'Now, to you my lovely little miss.'

Nellie took Saskia's hand, and then there was silence, but both Saskia and Nellie were exchanging expressions.

'Out loud please, girls,' James said and suddenly broke the silence.

'Sorry,' said Nellie, 'she placed her voice in my head effortlessly.' Nellie looked very surprised at this. 'Her power is already very strong. I feel it running through me.' She paused. 'But she too has not experienced her full awakening. Saskia, I cannot tell you the type of witch you will be.'

Saskia nodded and her big blue eyes spread happiness and cheer around the room.

'I see the same explosion, but this time from a different angle. Zachary's awakening will trigger Saskia's. This is all I can say as the view I am getting is the centre of the blast. I cannot see its size, but I feel its power and, and . . . .'

'What do you see?' Jenna said sharply.

'How strong are you, my lovely?' Nellie directed this comment towards Jenna.

'For them, I can be as strong as I need to,' she said, straightening up and frowning.

'I feel your power stretch itself and expand as you say this. That's quite remarkable. How long can you do that, how far does it go?'

'Oh, er, I don't know really. I have never pushed for too long, but I always feel there is more.'

'That's most extraordinary. Most Protectors can feel the ceiling to their power, but not you. That's good because you are going to need it when these two Crack. Practice stretching and expanding your power quickly. It will help you on your journey.'

'I will.'

'And now to the smallest wizard of all. This one has been fully awakened. I could feel this long before we met in the market. To be honest, I could feel him enter the city and knew you were all close.'

She took his small hand. Immediately, she took in a large gulp of air and let go. Quickly releasing Rafi's hand, Nellie stared at Jenna and James with a look of shock.

A single tear ran down Jenna's face.

'What do you see, Nellie?' James said in a low, calm voice.

'This child has great power—beyond anything I have ever seen. He should not be here. You have brought danger to this city, and danger will travel wherever he goes.'

'I can contain him,' Jenna said firmly.

'You don't know your own limits, let alone his. How do you know this?'

'Because I must. I simply must shield him from the world and protect him until he can control his own strength.'

Nellie could feel the pain in Jenna, and as a mother herself, her empathy ran deep. She too began to shed tears.

'Even if you could protect this one powerful child, how will you protect the world from three Olympians?'

Once she had said it, the look on the parents' faces was one of shock and fear.

'No!' Jenna called out and held her face in her hands, hiding herself from the room.

James put his arm around her.

'Jenna, James, you must seek help in raising these children.'

'From who?' asked James.

'The Darwinians or the League of Olympians. One of these organisations must help you, or I fear for all mankind that history will repeat itself.'

'What do you mean by "history will repeat itself"?'

'I mean they will rule the world with tyranny.'

'No! You are wrong,' James said angrily. 'Have you seen this? Did that come to you?'

'I don't need to see it. These three Olympians must be contained.'

'But you have not seen it. This is only your opinion and not a vision, right?'

'You have been warned. You must seek help.'

'I will not join either group Nellie. You know that.'

'There are many ghosts within the League these days. These wizards are your friends, think about it.'

James nodded.

Suddenly, a rasping sound came from Rafi as he let off the most gigantic amount of wind.

'Yummy, chocolate pops.' He giggled whilst chewing the sweets.

Everyone started laughing as the child's antics broke the serious and threatening mood—everyone apart from Jenna, who remained stone-faced.

Chapter 9: A Night at the Rodeo

The temperature had cooled in the Lost City that evening and a wind blew in from the west, ruffling people's hair and causing mischief with all the campers' equipment. The campers themselves now filled a large section of the open green area that led off into the jungle. The deserted market channel and makeshift canopy remained where the thriving market had been, with all the day's litter tied up in large black sacks outside each empty stall.

'He can't be that hard to see, he's a giant bald Cyclops with tattoos all over his head—can't be too many of those around tonight,' said James, walking through the party atmosphere of the campers and the plethora of camping equipment.

'Nellie said he'd be near the edge because he can see over everyone's heads,' replied Jenna.

'Yeah, but knowing him, he got a prime spot for the kids to see.'

'Yeah, he seems so nice and gentle!' she shouted over a lively barbeque in full flow, attended by lots of people who were cheering and laughing.

The children walked again in wonder, looking at the people flying overhead, the mysterious-looking characters, and the creatures around the campsites. A woman called to her son, who was around Zachary's age, to light the campfire. The boy smiled at Zachary and took out a long white wand and shot a bolt into a pile of wood that immediately burst into high flames.

'Cool,' said Zachary.

The boy smiled at his fire and then walked back to his mother. Meanwhile, Jenna was feeling claustrophobic walking through the tightly packed people again.

'Right! Wait here,' she called out.

James and the children watched as she took off and flew all around the large camping area. A few minutes later, she was back.

'He's over there.' She pointed to the far edge of the site. 'We couldn't see him because he is sitting around a fire, drinking with his sons, Mark, and a really, really big guy who looks like a sumo wrestler.'

'Skinny's here? Brilliant!' exclaimed James.

'Skinny?' said Saskia with a look of amusement.

'Yeah, it's ironic.' She looked confused. 'It's kind of a joke on his size.'

'Ah, I get it daddy.'

Jenna grabbed the nearest of her children and took off. James followed with Rafi. They flew up to a high point so as not to interrupt anyone's evening, and then swooped down to a gentle landing in an opening next to the group of men and their tents. It soon became obvious why there was an empty patch in such a tightly packed camping area. The men were being very loud and playful with each other, probably down to the drink they were packing away. Their size and noise were enough to put most people off being near them.

'Crikey! Sounds like a rugby match over here,' James called out over the deep laugh of Gwion and his boys as he pushed Mark backwards over the log he was sitting on. He landed directly at Jenna's feet, face up. He noticed Jenna's look of disapproval.

'Hello gorgeous,' he said through a muffled giggle.

'Don't you "gorgeous" me. I know your type, Mark Anthony,' she said with a half-amused look on her face.

'Aw, don't be like that. Surely being married to James makes you appreciate a handsome guy like me?'

They all burst out laughing at this.

'And so the evening begins,' James said through a laugh and shaking his head.

A massive man resembling a giant sumo wrestler pulled his great weight to his feet and stood strong at six foot five inches tall, wearing a serious expression on his deadpan oriental features. He had a very wide nose, dark skin, and thick eyebrows that were showing a deep frown. He thudded over to stand directly in front of James and the two stared at each other for what appeared to be an eternity. The massive man very gradually stretched his mouth into a broad smile and suddenly threw his arms out at either side, frightening the children with his quick movement. He grabbed James in a giant bear hug, pinning his arms to his sides and lifting him from the ground, all while pushing his face into James's chest like a child cuddling his favourite teddy. He released a hand and patted James's back with three giant thuds, making James wince with each contact.

'Where have you been all this time?' the big man called out.

'Hey Skinny,' James wheezed through the hug, 'I missed you too.'

Skinny put him down and looked at Jenna and the children, making them feel uncomfortable.

'Jenna, kids, this is Hirotomi Tsunemori, also known as "Skinny". He helped me many years ago and is the longest living ghost I know of.'

'Very pleased to meet you.' Jenna put out her hand.

'Pleased to meet you,' he repeated. 'You are very beautiful.'

'Oh, er, thank you,' Jenna said and blushed.

'Despite his age, we are still working on his social skills,' Mark called out from beside Skinny. Skinny reached out one massive hand, grabbed Mark by the face, and pushed him over, causing him to land on his bottom and make all the men laugh hysterically again. Skinny crouched down and looked intensely at the three children.

'Come, come.' He beckoned with a wave.

The children edged slowly towards the big man, reassured by James's happy expression while he watched them and nodded encouragement.

'Zachary,' Skinny said and he reached out, placing his hands on Zachary's shoulders and looking him directly in the eyes, 'I like you.' He smiled again.

Zachary smiled.

'You are a powerful Conjurer,' he continued, 'protect Skinny and frighten our enemies.'

Jenna raised an eyebrow and voiced in James's head, '*How does he know this?*'

'*It's hard to know exactly where he gets this stuff from. No one really knows how old he is or where it all began, but this man never ceases to amaze me—just go with it rather than trying to understand it. Oh, and he can hear everything we say,'* James replied.

Skinny tore his gaze away from Zachary's eyes for a split second to look at Jenna and wink. Jenna blushed awkwardly.

'Zachary and Skinny, become good friends and look after each other, yes?' Skinny said seriously.

'Ok,' answered Zachary.

'Great! High five.' Skinny reached his hand high and Zachary slapped it.

Then he moved his great size to face Saskia.

'Saskia, come, come.' He waved her forwards again.

She moved to stand next to Zachary, and again, he placed his massive hands on her tiny shoulders, making her look like a small dolly in front of him.

'Oh! You are powerful Healer,' he said. 'You fix Skinny when he is broken.'

Saskia beamed at this news.

'You are also very beautiful,' he continued, 'Skinny protect Saskia from boys when you start courting.'

'Suits me,' James pitched in.

'High five!' Skinny raised his hand again and Saskia jumped up and smacked it. Skinny pretended this hurt him and she giggled and moved back to stand beside her mother.

'You. Come.' Skinny said as he pointed at Rafi.

Rafi moved forwards and puffed out his chest.

'Skinny likes Rafi very much,' he said, placing his hands on the even smaller set of shoulders.

Rafi puffed up to make himself as big as possible before the massive man. He looked at him with reverence and admiration because of the immense size and strength he possessed.

'Oooh! He has awakened.' Skinny directed his comment towards James, tearing his gaze away from Rafi's eyes for a second. He looked back at Rafi and hunched down lower whilst still crouching to bring his eyes directly into Rafi's gaze. Skinny continued to look deep into Rafi's eyes, as if trying to see something that was hiding.

'Excellent! Rafi, you are strong Warrior like Skinny.'

Rafi beamed and smiled at his Daddy, happy that they were all the same.

'Rafi and Skinny fight alongside each other. We look after each other, yes?'

Rafi nodded.

'Great! High five.'

Rafi leapt up about twelve feet in the air and performed a perfect backwards somersault, slapping the massive hand, and wearing a look of surprise on his own face during his descent.

'Blimey!' said Zachary.

Skinny stood to his full height and looked at Jenna and James.

'Skinny will help you. We will look after them together,' he said.

'Thank you, old friend,' said James.

'Hey, we are all in this together,' said Gwion, moving to stand near Skinny and facing Jenna and James as well.

'That's right,' pitched in Patrick and Grub.

'Ghosts stick together,' Mark said, moving into the huddle to stand before the family.

'Thank you my old friends, this means everything to me,' said James.

Jenna blinked away tears of happiness, finally feeling strength on her side for the first time in days.

'Ghosts and devils, Dad?' Saskia folded her arms and looked at James quizzically.

'Anyone thirsty?' James directed at the group of men.

They agreed in unison and turned back to their campfire. James turned to Saskia.

'Let's get set up here for the evening and then have a chat around the campfire.'

She nodded and Jenna grabbed her crystal from around her neck. The necklace wrapped itself around her hand and up her wrist with a life of its own, with the main largest crystal in her palm. She pointed her hand to the open space next to the men who were now drinking and casting the occasional look at the family. James took the pencil from behind his ear and the children watched its fibres come to life and grow into his large staff. Once it was taller than him, he pointed it to the same spot as Jenna and he nodded, indicating that he was ready.

They both stood firm and flexed their muscles as a mist rose from the ground and vapour poured in from all angles until a thick cloud-like fog filled the area and a shadow formed slowly within. The process took over two minutes. As the mist started to dissipate, the children could see a small log cabin forming, as if being drawn in three dimensions with an invisible spray can. The mist shrank down to leave the little cabin, complete with wooden door and two lattice windows on either side of it, standing before them. Jenna pushed her arm out again and a flash of light came from within the cabin. Its small chimney started letting out a plume of smoke.

'Perfect,' said Jenna.

'That was brilliant!' said Zachary.

'Yes, but what takes two wizards five minutes can be done in an instant with one great Conjurer.' James said nudging his son, watching the excitement rise on his face.

'I can't wait until my Dawn', he said.

'All in good time, sunshine.'

'What's this?' came a high-pitched call from Gwion. 'What's wrong with a good, old-fashioned tent?'

'I don't do tents,' said Jenna.

'You and me are going to get along just fine,' came the voice of Nellie, who was flying in gently from behind the group.

Gwion waved at them as if to blow off their sentiment and joined the men again.

'I'll stay for the rodeo and then I'm off to my lovely comfortable house. Care to join me?' Nellie asked Jenna. 'There's a piping hot shower and double bed with your name on it.'

'That would be lovely, thank you.' Jenna beamed.

'Er, what about us and having a family adventure?' said James.

'I think we have had enough of a family adventure, don't you? Time for some rest and relaxation. It's not like there is no one to look out for the children with three devils and three Cyclopes around.'

'She's right you know,' Mark called out.

'Four of them being ghosts,' Nellie pitched in.

'Yes, thank you Mark, Nellie.' James shot them a look of 'mind your own business'. 'Fine, go chill out. You deserve it. I'll fill the kids in on the missing pieces.'

'You'll enjoy that.' Jenna smiled.

'Oooh! Look out, here they come!' Gwion called out and a hush settled over the campers' party atmosphere. Heads started to popup above the small cabins and tents that filled almost every gap in the large green field.

An official-looking man wearing a three-piece suit and large golden chain around his neck, creating the effect of a mayor's costume, walked out onto the open field that had been sectioned away from the campers. People started to cheer and a flock of last minute spectators flew in, having been signalled by their companions. He took out a megaphone and addressed the audience.

'Good evening wizards, witches, and all those with magic in their blood!' This was the standard greeting for a magical crowd, and they erupted into applause.

'This evening, we have a great line-up for you. We have a whole herd of fifteen—yes, fifteen—winged horses and some of the most famous riders in the circuit to tame them. You may have heard of some of these riders,' he teased the audience, 'like young Peter Flanagan from Xamenia, pixie Warrior Dauphine Grindal, and the foremost amongst them, the great Prince Nerdache.'

The crowd went wild with cheers.

'After a short interval, during which you can pick up refreshments at our fantastic stands, sponsored by our brothers at Darwinian Global . . .' He pointed to the stalls on the edge of the field and the sponsor banner that hung above them, showing a happy array of magical creatures reaching to shake the hand of a smiling man in a black suit. There was stuttered applause and a few uncomfortable boos '. . . We will continue the second half of the show in complete silence.'

The audience went wild again, knowing the reason for the silence.

'Settle down, settle down now. Yes, as I was saying, we will continue the second half in complete silence as the Brotherhood of Centaurs brings out a herd of unicorns for our riders to risk their very lives on for your entertainment.'

The crowd practically exploded with applause and screams over the excitement of unicorn riding.

'So, without further delay, may I welcome for your entertainment, young Peter Flanagan!'

He gestured to an opening in the jungle where a large spotlight suddenly shone and the audience went silent. There was a pause of two minutes, making the crowd start to fidget with anticipation.

Suddenly, a massive pure white stallion bigger than any shire horse burst through the foliage and out from the trees, roughly thirty feet in the air, with its gigantic wings fully spread and muscles rippling. Its small rider was almost impossible to see and looked like a child on top of the wild beast. The horse was fierce with rage, obviously never having been ridden before, and it swooped around the sky at breakneck speed, bucking and kicking in all directions, trying desperately to shake its rider, who was putting up a valiant effort to stay on top.

The horse swooped towards the ground. Everyone held their breath as it looked like it was set to crash into the earth before them. Just when the collision seemed inevitable the horse's beautiful wings spread full, allowing it to perform a perfect swoop just above the heads of the crowd, who went wild in awe of the spectacle just a whisker's length above them.

The excitement continued as the horse used its momentum to continue the swoop into a loop-the-loop. As the pair reached the peak of the second loop, the animal seemed to win the battle with a fantastic effort that paused them both at the crest, whilst upside down. With a flick of its tail, the horse caused poor Peter Flanagan to come clean away and he started to fall. The crowd inhaled with horror, not knowing Peter's flying ability, if he had any at all. The horse did not merely levitate in mid-air, its fabulous wings also started to beat to control its own fall. It twisted and contorted its giant body, clearly struggling to get control from its incredible stunt and with a big effort managed to turn its fall into a dive, which took it past the falling Peter Flanagan.

Flanagan reacted immediately and folded his body into a ball, causing him to fall faster. Then he manoeuvred himself into a straight line with his hands pressed in tightly by his sides. The two were falling at an incredible pace. The horse was clearly building up speed to make a fast escape, unaware of the determined rodeo star right behind him, watching his every move. Just as it looked like Flanagan would catch up to the horse and was within a few feet, without warning, he spread his arms and legs, causing him to slow and move away from the falling beast. The angle at which he was falling shifted to be above the horse. It suddenly became clear why Flanagan had done this and it demonstrated to the audience why he was such a big rodeo star. The horse reached its top speed and fully spread its wings once again, causing yet another plummet that ended with a sharp swoop that led it right into Flanagan's path. Flanagan had prepared for this and had his legs wide open to catch the horse between them.

The crowd erupted in celebration and the horse had no option but to continue the swoop it was performing, but now with the rider firmly in place again. Once out of the swoop, the horse once again began to buck and kick in desperation to throw Flanagan, but it seemed all of its previous efforts had taken their toll and the horse's energy seemed to be running out. The ride continued for another five minutes before the horse had clearly had enough and Flanagan knew that he needed to rest and give way to the next act, so he performed an incredible back flip dismount as soon as the horse bought him over the green area before the crowd.

Once he landed, he performed a low bow and the crowd applauded and whooped with fervour. The horse came to a landing behind him and trotted to a halt, whereupon two fauns came running out and placed a bucket of water before the beast and then retreated quickly. The horse drank and Peter directed the crowd's attention with an outstretched arm towards the steed. They applauded once again at the spectacle they had witnessed and for the true showmanship of Peter Flanagan.

'Blimey he's good. Isn't he?' Mark said to James whilst nudging him.

'Crikey, you're not kidding! And that is one hell of a big horse,' said James.

'That was amazing!' Rafi cried out, being woken from his daze of excitement by the new conversation. The group all laughed and agreed.

'What's next?' asked Zachary.

'More of the same, but with different horses and riders,' Jenna answered.

'I feel a bit sorry for the horse. I think he doesn't like it,' Saskia said to Jenna.

'This one has to be a Healer,' Nellie whispered in Jenna's ear, referring to Saskia.

'I hope so. Wouldn't that be wonderful?'

Nellie nodded.

The entertainment continued for another hour and the crowd was wowed with more giant horses and brave riders, some even being thrown clear off their rides with no hope of return—but all the participants landed safely. A short break was announced by the official-looking man in the three-piece suit and he took great pleasure in reminding the audience of the acts they had just seen, causing yet more applause. Then he pointed out the sponsor once again and the banner above the refreshment stands.

'Let's hear it for our kind sponsor, who has laid out refreshments on such a lovely and exciting evening!'

A few people clapped, and again there were a few anonymous boos.

'Our brothers at Darwinian Global everybody!' he chirped again.

He looked very awkward standing in the face of such a lack in enthusiasm.

'Why doesn't anyone like the Darwinian Global people?' Saskia asked her mother.

All conversations stopped around the campfire to listen to her response.

'Darwinian Global is a very big and powerful company that tries to manage wizarding activity around the world. The problem is that no one voted them in, and the wizarding world doesn't like being told what to do. We have had a hard enough time in history without some of our own kind now telling us what we can and can't do.'

'People are scared of their great power,' James added.

'The League keeps them in check,' said Mark with a wink.

'You didn't join the League of Olympians Mark, did you?' asked James.

Mark looked around awkwardly and shifted in his seat.

'Maybe I did. I met the leader, Rufus, not long ago and he seemed pretty straight down the line to me.'

'By "straight down the line" do you mean he has a superiority complex, a need for anarchy and a loathing of non-wizards?'

'Yeah, something like that, apart from the anarchy bit—unless you are a Darwinian. He's really down on them.'

'Brilliant! Another bloody war, Mark, that's exactly what we need.'

'Yeah, well, as you have seen, those Darwinians are getting too strong and somebody needs to keep them in line.'

'Shut up, you two, or I'll smash your heads together,' called out Gwion.

James shot Mark a look of disgust and Mark threw his arms out as if saying 'What did I do wrong?'

'On that cheery note, I think I'll take my leave and let you gentlemen and lady,' Nellie curtsied to Saskia, 'enjoy the rest of the evening without me. Are you coming?' Nellie asked Jenna.

'Definitely!' she replied.

'But we are only halfway through and there's a herd of unicorns coming out—real unicorns!' James said in disbelief to the fact that they were leaving.

'I'm afraid a hot shower and a safe comfy bed trumps your unicorn, my love, but you stay and enjoy with the kids,' Jenna said whilst stroking James's hair as he sat on a log before her around the campfire.

'Suit yourself,' James said grumpily.

'Goodnight, my darlings.' Jenna went around the campfire and kissed her children.

'What? No kiss for me?' said Mark with a cheeky grin.

Jenna blew him a kiss and James rolled his eyes at Skinny, who was giggling at Mark's flirtatious behaviour.

'Goodnight everyone. You boys keep an eye on those kids,' Nellie said sternly to the group of men sitting in the circle around the fire. She thought inwardly what a picture of strength they made and that it would take an army to beat them.

Nellie and Jenna took off and flew away in the direction of the cottage.

'Right, now that the women have gone, let's break out the good stuff!' said Gwion, holding out an old-looking bottle.

'Erm, excuse me,' said Saskia.

'Oh, sorry me love, I meant now that the bossy women have gone and my favourite is here, we can bring out the good stuff.'

'That's better.' She winked at the giant Cyclops.

Everyone giggled and the evening kicked off loudly with the men making fun of each other and telling old stories. The feeling in the campsite was electric, filled with sounds of laughter and songs coming from all over. The added excitement of the rodeo kept people going.

Saskia nudged Zachary to call his attention to some new arrivals that had just turned up at the edge of the fence and were proceeding to line themselves up by sitting on its top rung. They were tiny little men wearing only a small piece of brown cloth to cover their pride and many exotic looking necklaces. They looked like native tribesmen, but were each only about two feet tall and grubby, with long black hair styled into all kinds of large shapes. The children thought they looked funny and Rafi pointed at them while they were pushing and shoving each other for positions on the fence.

As if to make the children laugh even more, they started to fight amongst themselves for seating positions, even though the fence went for many hundreds of metres and there were only about fifteen of them present. They all wanted to sit in one particular section and started pushing each other off. Those that had seated themselves near the edge and had avoided the fighting started to laugh at their own party with a very high-pitched giggle that caused the children to laugh even louder.

The spectator tribesmen went into hysterics as the fighting went into overdrive and they started hitting each other over the head with the small clubs they carried. Suddenly, the fighting men stopped and looked at the six hysterically giggling tribesmen sitting on the end of the fence and collectively seemed to be very annoyed at being laughed at. They all leapt into the air and landed on the laughing tribesmen and started fighting them, too.

James and the others had the closest campsite to this spectacle and they were all giggling whilst watching the little men fighting and laughing at each other. They were so small and fast and laughed in such high-pitched giggles that everyone watching the scene unfold, laughed even harder.

'They are so funny!' Rafi said loudly, pointing at the crowd of fighting and giggling little men.

They all stopped suddenly and looked around in the direction of the voice with anger on their little faces. James jumped up immediately and held his hands high, as if surrendering, and approached the group. A few of them leapt onto the top rung of the fence and started animatedly shouting at James in their high-pitched voices, all the while pointing at Rafi. James continued his discussion with them for a few minutes, repeating his apology for insulting them.

'What's going on?' whispered Zachary into Mark's ear.

Mark leaned in and the three children huddled around him.

'Those are Nachawai pigmy tribesmen. They are extremely volatile.' He stopped, noticing the confused look on Rafi's face. 'It means they get angry quite quickly.' Rafi nodded. 'Whilst they are known for fighting amongst themselves, they think nothing of attacking anyone or anything. Their bravery goes well beyond their size. However, they look, act, and sound very funny, which often causes people to point or say something slightly offensive. Such things can give them the excuse to attack.'

'You mean, like Rafi just did?' said Saskia.

Rafi opened his eyes wide and his head fell.

'Hey, don't worry kiddo. You weren't to know,' Mark said, ruffling Rafi's hair and making him brighten up.

'Are we in danger?' asked Zachary.

Mark smiled broadly.

'You're kidding! Between us Warriors, we have the power of an army sitting around this campfire. Your dad is saving them from a painful ending. Sit back and enjoy the entertainment, I say.'

Gwion and Grub shifted around the campfire to sit closer to the children.

'Yeah, this could get funny. Watch the littlest fella at the far left on the ground,' said Gwion.

'He's been secretly taking out a blowpipe from his waistband,' Grub interjected.

'We should warn Dad.' Zachary suddenly sounded alarmed.

'He already did, but Dad knows,' responded Saskia.

'You were listening, right, blue eyes?' Mark said to Saskia.

She blushed at his directness accompanied by his good looks.

They all sat back and watched the unexpected entertainment when the main pigmy arguing with James slammed his club down on the fence in anger, knocking a few of his tribesmen off in the process and causing the ones left on the fence to burst into high-pitched hysterics. Everyone around the campfire and the crowd that had now started watching with craned necks from various places in the campsite started giggling again. This made the main pigmy go bright red. Veins started standing up on his little neck as he squealed at James, who remained calm, still holding his hands up in surrender.

The pigmy could not stand it anymore and swung his club back.

'This should be good,' said Gwion through a toothy grin.

The pigmy jumped up above James's head and swung the club down with the large end aimed straight at James's skull. James caught the club with his right hand without much effort and held both the club and the attached pigmy in mid-flight. The sound of a sharp blow alerted everyone to the pigmy on the floor with the blow dart and they could see he had aimed directly at James. James had raised his left hand and caught the dart between his thumb and forefinger before it struck.

'Awesome!' said Rafi.

The pigmies looked at the dart and their leader in mid-flight and gathered themselves up, raising their weapons.

'Come on, before this gets bloody,' said Gwion, standing to his full height and puffing out his chest.

The other men also stood at this signal and stared at the angry pigmy tribesmen. James sensed the men rise behind him and knew that Mark, Skinny, Grub, Patrick, and Gwion would be an awesome sight to behold.

The tribesmen peered around James at the giants, then suddenly huddled into a circle. Their leader still hung in the air and screamed at them to attack. The huddle broke up and the group looked up at their leader. One of them pointed at him and laughed hysterically, causing the others to follow suit. This broke the stiff atmosphere and everyone relaxed.

The men all sat down, while the pigmies lined themselves up on the top rung of the fence and re-seated, waving James away as if to say 'Don't worry about it'. James put the pigmy leader down on the fence, who ignored the gesture of kindness and proceeded to shout at his men.

James turned and looked at his children, shrugged, and then walked back.

'That was fun,' he said.

'Sorry Dad,' said a repentant-looking Rafi.

'Hey, no problem Raf, you weren't to know.' He leaned closer to his youngest son and whispered, 'Besides, they are only little fellas.'

They both laughed.

The voice of the man in the smart three-piece suit came booming out from the field.

'Welcome back everyone, I trust you enjoyed your refreshments, courtesy of Darwinian Global!'

He paused and started to applaud, but no one followed his example, so his clapping slowed and then stopped. Coughing to break the silence, he continued his introduction.

'We have an incredibly exciting second half for you. I have been informed during the interval, whilst tucking into my fantastic refreshments,' he paused and looked sheepish at another attempt to promote the unpopular sponsor, 'that the Brotherhood of Centaurs has successfully herded the unicorns to the forest edge, where they will lead them onto the field one at a time. From there, our brave riders will first attempt to mount them, and then, if they have not been speared, they will attempt to ride them for as long as they can hold on.'

The crowd erupted with a cheer.

'As you all know, unicorns are incredibly shy creatures, so we will bring out our Protectors in a minute to shield the crowd from sight and sound. However, we still ask that you stay completely silent as a precaution to our riders. Thank you very much and let's bring on the protectors.'

Two men and a woman came out of the wooded opening, all wearing black suits, white shirts, and black ties, signifying that they were part of Darwinian Global. This realisation caused the crowd to fall into an eerie silence. The three walked to stand in front of the crowd, facing them with blank stern expressions on their faces. They positioned themselves around thirty feet away from the edge of the encampment. Then they raised their right hands in unison and slowly waved them down over the crowd, causing a large blue half-dome to appear and fade out over the crowded area. The dome disappeared and the booming voice of the three-piece suit came back.

'The shield is now in place. Let's hear it for the lovely people at Darwinian Global once more—what a great job they did.'

He was the only person to clap and the three Darwinians remained cold faced. They bowed to the crowd, stood up straight, and walked off back in the direction they had come from.

'Right then,' continued the man in the three-piece suit, 'without further delay, let the games begin!'

There was complete silence in the city and darkness in the field beyond the campsite. People were craning their necks to look into the forest, hoping to catch a glimpse of movement. A soft glow of light grew from deep within the trees and gradually got stronger and stronger until a large centaur came into view. He was very muscular and had wild long golden hair and a beard to match. His horse hair matched the colour of his human hair and he was a sight to behold coming out of the jungle, only visible due to the bright glow that followed him. As he trotted out, the glow grew to become a bright light and the audience let out a collective quiet 'Oooh' as a white stallion came trotting out of the trees.

Like the centaur before him, the unicorn was extremely muscly, but with a coat of pure white and a long white horn in the centre of his nose. He was emanating light, making his arrival even more magical and the effect of the two characters on the campsite was electric.

A dark figure flew out of the trees from the same point where the unicorn had exited and circled high above the pair below, causing the unicorn to stir and twitch slightly. The dark figure hung in the air above them, faced the audience, and bowed. Then he held his left hand high and counted down from five with his fingers. The excitement was unbearable and people fidgeted and hid behind their hands as they watched in silence. As the dark figure reached one, he threw his arms and legs out to make a star shape and let himself drop to the unicorn beneath him. He landed squarely on its back, which caused the beast to go wild.

The centaur, realising the dark figure's intentions, headed out to the edge of the field at a fast gallop and all eyes fell on the bucking unicorn and the dark character hanging on for dear life. There was a sudden pop and the pair disappeared only to reappear twenty metres away, still in a wild bucking fury. Then again, there was a pop and the pair disappeared and reappeared in a different section of the field. This happened several times, but still the rider clung tight. Then the unicorn changed tactics and there was a machine gun fire of popping, with the beast disappearing and reappearing faster than the audience could watch. This disoriented the rider, as intended, and the unicorn, sensing this, let out a giant buck that flung the rider clear off his back and high above the unicorn's head.

As the rider came down, the beast rammed his head high, thrusting the long and sharp point of the horn towards the falling body. The audience held their breath and children hid their faces behind their hands. The rider must have caught sight of the fearful horn, and just as the point was inches away from his body, he twisted in the air and performed a flip that only just moved him out of the way of a gruesome death. He landed just beyond the unicorn and quickly ran away from the wild beast.

The unicorn gave chase and it was clear that the rider would not last long zigzagging around the path of the thrusting horn. The centaur re-entered the field in a gallop and rode close to the rider, offering him a strong arm. The rider grabbed the centaur's arm and somersaulted himself up onto it's back, and the pair rode away from the unicorn, who came to an abrupt halt.

The audience went wild and cheered the brave rider whilst watching the unicorn twitch and bluster before them. The rider jumped from the centaur's back once they were a safe distance away and took a long deep bow, causing more applause. He threw his arm out towards the unicorn in the field before him, calling applause for the beast, which the campers obliged accompanied with whoops and cheers that grew even louder. The crowd slowly fell back into silence, the unicorn blustered some more and let out a loud whinny, standing high on his back legs in a graceful protest at being ridden. Then, with a loud pop, he disappeared.

'That was brilliant!' screamed Rafi.

'Daddy, we should do this every night,' Saskia added.

'They are not here every night—only when unicorns can be found nearby. The rodeo travels wherever unicorns are spotted and there haven't been any in these parts for eight years,' Mark responded.

'Where's the next one?' asked Zachary.

'No one knows. That's why they are so popular. But don't worry, it's not over yet,' said Patrick.

'Yeah, I can guarantee that there will be blood before the night is out,' said Grub morbidly with a grin.

'Really?' asked Saskia, clearly beginning to worry.

'Yes baby girl, someone usually gets hurt. It's very dangerous work, riding unicorns, but normally it's not deadly.'

Saskia cuddled into James as the next unicorn was led out in silence and another daring act took place. The night passed quickly with all the excitement and the crowd revelling in the games.

'Reminds me of the Roman games in the Colosseum,' Mark said to the group.

'Except the participants have a choice this time,' said James.

'I fought hard for that right in the past.'

'You did, my friend. We should celebrate that with more drink.' James grinned and topped up Mark's cup.

'To lost friends!' Mark toasted.

The others all repeated his toast, looked solemn for a moment, and then drank. The group of men got louder as the entertainment drew to a close and they all got drunk, aside from James, who continually reminded himself of his babysitting duties and lightly touched his beer every so often.

The man in the three-piece suit came out and gave a closing speech. Most people applauded until he made his last ditch attempt to warm them towards Darwinian Global when once again the crowd went silent. He gave up and blustered on, thanking his riders to massive applause.

The crowd was still very excited as the lights on the field were snuffed out, leaving only the campfires to cast a warm glow over the thousands of campers. The dying light calmed the crowd as people prepared themselves for bed, and at nearly one o'clock in the morning, most people settled down quickly, with only the hardened drinkers whispering and conspiring in the darkness, accompanied by an occasional burst of laughter.

James stood and announced to the group that they would be going to bed.

'What? Nooo!' slurred Gwion. 'The night is still young.'

He hiccupped and everyone laughed at him. Skinny laughed his loud deep belly laugh and hit Gwion on the back, causing him to fall off his log again. This put the men in fits of silent laughter and caused tears to stream down their faces. James rolled his eyes at them for his children's benefit.

'Come on kids, let's test out our cabin,' James said, standing and moving off. The children were tired and keen to camp in their new little house, so they did not need much encouragement.

The cabin had one tiny room, just big enough for five people to lie down in the middle, and was complete with a small fireplace on one wall and a working toilet and basin on another. There were five sleeping bags in the centre and the children all stripped down to their underwear, took it in turns to use the toilet, wash their hands and face and brush their teeth. The three children all snuggled up close to one another in their sleeping bags and James was all set to tuck them in and head back outside to re-join the other men when Saskia bolted upright.

'Daddy, you promised us an explanation about what happened with Mark and his tail!' she said indignantly.

'So I did, princess.'

James sat down at the end of their sleeping bags and the boys both sat up.

'Ok, so you know what Warriors are and that I am one. Plus you know that times have not always been easy for wizards in the world,' he began and the children nodded along. 'Well, today, you heard some wizards being called "ghosts" and I am one of those too.'

The children raised their eyebrows and James continued, '"ghost" is more of a nickname for a magical condition. It means that I am very powerful magically, and that because of this power within me, I will live for a long, long time. That's where the nickname comes from. Have you ever heard of the saying, "You look like you have seen a ghost"?'

The children nodded, but James was not convinced Rafi knew what he was talking about.

'Well, that saying means you look like you got a fright from seeing someone you thought was dead. When you are a ghost wizard, you live so long that eventually you will bump into others in the wizarding cities who may have seen you when they were children. Such people get a shock because they've grown up, but you haven't changed. Hence, they "look like they have seen a ghost". Get it?'

The children nodded.

'Will I live a long, long time Daddy?' asked Saskia, who was much more awake than the boys.

'Perhaps my darling, you three will be ghosts too, as both your parents are—although Mum isn't officially a ghost until her hundredth birthday.'

'Mummy's a ghost too?' Saskia beamed.

'Not officially, but her magical strength is incredible and Nellie gave her the title in her last reading, so the chances of you three being powerful enough to be ghosts is likely.'

'That so cool,' said Zachary and the others agreed.

'What about Mark's tail?' Saskia said incredulously.

'Nothing gets past you, does it, my little dragon?'

Saskia smiled and James sat back down.

'This one may be a little harder for you to accept. When you are a ghost, you have greater power within you than most wizards. Mark, Skinny, Gwion, and I are all ghosts, although I expect Patrick and Grub are too, just not officially yet. What you saw today was a unique transformation that happens with ghost Warriors only. During battles, we have the ability to transform our appearance to strike fear into our enemies. Unfortunately, this ability is not always voluntary, and when we experience fear or threat, it may happen on its own.'

'What happens to you, Daddy?'

'Well, it's a similar transformation for most of us. We grow in size, change colour all over—even our eyes—we grow a tail like the one you saw on Mark today, and sometimes we grow horns and fangs.'

'Fangs!' Saskia frowned.

'Yes, generally, we look terrifying. Coupled with our fighting ability and long life, this means that ghosts have survived for centuries. This is also why people are often scared of us and call us devils.'

'Oh, that's why the leprechaun was mean to you both today.'

'Yes, he had pixies in those little black cases and they are very sensitive to ghosts.'

'What colour do you go?'

'I go bright red and look just like pictures of the devil. I hope that you will never see me like that.' He paused. 'I'm not dangerous to you though. I'm completely me, just ready to fight, and all my senses have gone off the scale.'

'I like red,' said Saskia, putting positivity into the conversation.

'Thank you, baby girl.' He stroked her face. 'Right, now it is time for sleep.'

James looked over at the boys. Zachary was already drifting off and Rafi had already fallen asleep.

'Daddy?'

'Yes Saskia?'

'I wish Mummy was here to say goodnight.'

'Well, why don't we practice your newfound ability and send her a message?'

'Ok, what do I do?'

James sat opposite Saskia on the floor. They were both cross-legged and holding hands.

'I want you to focus your mind on listening to all the voices out there. Can you do that for me?'

She nodded and closed her eyes.

'Think of all the voices out there and listen to them,' he continued.

'I hear them Daddy. It sounds like an old-fashioned radio that is receiving lots of stations at once.'

'Yes, that's it. Now, think of Mummy and really try and feel her. Think of her voice, smell, and touch.'

'I think I can feel her.'

'Great, say goodnight to her then.'

Saskia closed her eyes really tight and creases appeared around her face.

'I hear her!' she said excitedly.

'What's she saying?'

'She is saying "Goodnight, baby girl," and telling me off for being up so late.'

'That's amazing, my darling. Even I couldn't do that at this distance.'

'She says there are six Warriors in total, including ghosts and Cyclopes. "Attack formation alpha three, on my mark".'

Saskia frowned, not understanding what her mother had just said. James leapt to his feet immediately. He knew what this meant.

'Saskia, listen to me carefully.'

Saskia opened her eyes and was afraid.

'Tell Mummy they are coming. They are coming now, and she must get here. Can you do that my darling?'

She nodded and closed her eyes tight. After a few seconds, a single tear ran down her face.

'Mummy said, "Oh, God, please no!" and then told me to be strong and that she would be here in a few minutes.'

'You did well, baby girl, thank you.'

James squeezed her hands.

'What now Daddy?'

'Now, we fight. Wake the boys for me.' James stepped out and looked up at the sky. 'Warriors!' he shouted. 'I call you to arms, my brothers.'

There was a short pause and then came the response.

'I accept your call, my brother,' came Mark's voice.

Saskia could see a flash of light outside, and then she heard giant footsteps approach her father. A dark shadow was cast over James and he looked up at whoever had just approached. An extremely large bright red hand with black claws rested on James's back, coming down from a great height.

'I am ready,' came a very low deep voice.

'They will be here any second. It's the Darwinians, Saskia heard them signalling the attack formation.'

Another giant shadow thudded up to the cabin.

'Skinny accepts the call', came another very deep, low voice.

Then another three flashes of light went off and it sounded like a herd of giants was walking up and a single voice called out, 'We three accept your call, my brother.'

'We have no Protector, so the children will need to be defended directly. I fear the battle will begin after her arrival, so we will begin with opposing defence positions around me.

Move in to strike and then withdraw to maintain the defensive line. Understood?'

No response was given, but the shadows moved off and Saskia could hear them surrounding the house.

'What's happening Dad?' asked a sleepy Zachary.

'We are going to be attacked any second and I have called in my friends to help.'

He knelt down by Rafi and Saskia holding their hands.

'Remember how we were just talking about ghost Warriors and how they transform into really scary-looking big beasts?'

They all nodded.

'Right, well, all our friends outside, Mark, Skinny, Gwi, Patrick and Grub, have transformed and are defending us right now.'

James looked down at his feet.

'I will change too, but remember, I'm still your dad and we won't hurt you. I love you—we just look really scary.'

Someone outside screamed.

'Devil Warriors! Run for cover!'

Others started calling out.

'What's going on?' came a man's voice from far away.

'Look, devil Warriors!'

'Be brave, my babies. I'll be right back,' said James.

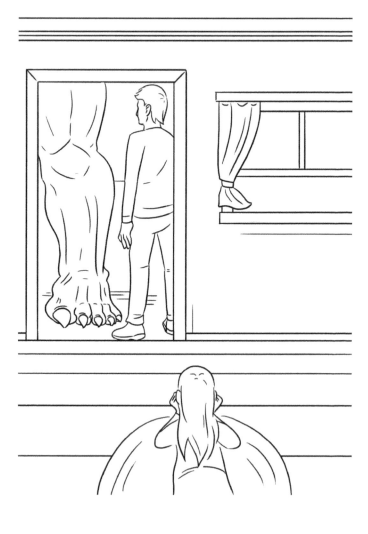

James stepped outside and the children shielded their eyes as a flash of light came from him. He glowed as if lit up from the inside by a light bulb. The light dimmed and he grew rapidly beyond the view of the children outside the front door. All they could see were his clothes ripping off and his now giant leg. Then a large red tail came flicking into view with a triangular black tip.

'Everyone here in the campsite, listen to me now!' bellowed a deep low voice that sounded like something from a fairy tale. The voice continued, 'There is about to be a battle here. You must go now to safety away from here—the Darwinians are coming.'

It sounded like a riot outside to the children, with people screaming and shouting and all kinds of crashes and bangs that sounded like the hasty collection of belongings. They could hear screams to run and hurry from all angles. Then came the voice again.

'Here they come, my brothers. Fight hard and take no prisoners,' James said in his deep fairy-tale rumble.

'See you in hell, brothers,' came another deep giant ghost Warrior voice.

'Aye!' came a chorus of giant shouts.

There was an explosion near the cabin that sounded like thunder and the children jumped and huddled together holding hands. There were several more thunderclaps and many flashes of light from directly outside the windows.

'Left flank, Mark,' came a booming voice.

'Got them,' came the unrecognisable deep voice that must have been Mark.

A giant clap of thunder came from outside and the ground shook, followed by screams of pain from people high up. More thunder and crashes came and the cabin shook louder and longer each time.

'I'm scared,' said Saskia.

'Me too,' said Rafi, starting to cry.

'Dad won't let anything happen to us. Come on you two,' Zachary said, confidently holding them both close, even though he was secretly very afraid. He ducked his head as another massive bang went off.

Then he pulled the other two children in tight as the windows blew in with a flash of lightning.

'Aaah!' shouted Zachary as glass rained on them.

'James, look up!' came the shout from another booming deep voice.

'Jesus! There's hundreds of them,' came James's deep rumble. 'Hold tight kids.'

The room was filled with light and Zachary closed his eyes and placed his hands instinctively on his siblings' heads, holding them tight and protecting their skulls. The cabin started shaking and vibrating constantly and cracks appeared all around them. Through the cracks came streams of light. The screams from people being injured or even killed came more rapidly now, accompanied by thunder and lightning just beyond the walls. There was a sudden gust within the cabin and the roof blew off in an instant.

Zachary held on to the other two children, but stuck his head up from the bundle and looked around. They were surrounded by five giant men with beastly features. There were four bright red beasts and one jet-black one. They were all at least twenty feet tall, with rippling muscles that pulsed and flexed as they fought the hundreds of people wearing black suits that were swooping down. The people attacking were of varying sizes, but they all were smaller than the beasts around them. They were swarming around the cabin like wasps to a nest, seemingly numbering in the thousands, and all were focussed on the giant nearest to them.

Zachary could make out who the giants were by their features. He noticed they were not that different from their normal selves, except for the fact that they were much, much bigger, with heavily exaggerated muscles, bright colouration, fangs, and dragon-like tails. Skinny was the biggest by a few feet and twice as wide as the second largest, plus he was the only one with jet-black skin and bright yellow eyes and hair. He was making easy work of smashing tens of Darwinians with every stroke and he held a bright white samurai sword. Flashes and explosions projected out towards wherever he pointed it. Then he used the sword to slash the air, causing vibrations and white streaks in the sky that were followed by screams in the distance.

Zachary turned and saw the two brothers working together back to back to cover each other. They were both holding medieval weapons. Grub was holding a bright yellow club and Patrick held a black weapon with a ball covered with spikes at the end. They both swung them around, smashing and killing the people flying about them. Grub was hit by a massive fireball that sent him flying over the children's heads. Zachary could make out a much larger Darwinian woman about ten feet tall in the spot where the fireball had come from. She was holding out a twig-like wand.

Immediately, Gwion took Grub's place and pushed out a bright blue glass-looking mallet that he held with two hands. The head was enormous, and from its tip came a blue swirl. It quickly turned into a massive blue fireball, looking like it was a blue bubble being blown out of fire. He gave a final push as it reached about the same size as him and it flew at breakneck speed into the Darwinian woman, who screamed, trying desperately to move and shield herself as the fireball vaporised her and at least fifty others in its path.

Grub was back on his feet, now covering the spot where his Dad had been in the circle around them, but he had a deep gash on his side that was weeping blood. Zachary could see that the wound was slowly healing before his eyes. He watched wide-eyed all about him while the giant Warriors were battling, killing, crushing, and occasionally being hit. As soon as they were hit, their bodies desperately began regenerating and healing, but the rate of injury was faster than their rate of regeneration. Slowly but surely, they were getting torn apart.

A loud clap of thunder above made him look up. He saw the massive crimson figure of his father tearing hundreds of Darwinians apart with broad strokes of his staff and powerful magic blasts. As the flashes of light came and then faded, Zachary would get a brief glimpse of his surroundings. He could see more swarms of Darwinians coming in at every angle in the swirl of the thunderstorm. *That's what this was*, he thought to himself, *it was a thunderstorm with no rain*. This was the reason his mother was always afraid of storms. It was not the actual storm she was afraid of, but the possibility that a battle such as this one was the source.

A massive thunderclap bought Zachary back to life and he watched Mark and his father working together, covering and calling each other's movements in the same way that the three Cyclopes were doing. Skinny worked alone, and to Zachary he seemed to be an unstoppable force. The Darwinians knew this, too, and Zachary watched them change tactics as the next wave shifted direction at the last minute. The people in black were like one being, and they flew in like the limb of a giant monster. They plunged into Skinny by the hundreds, covering him from head to toe and cutting into his mass of muscles. Zachary could see nothing of the monster underneath the black suits. It reminded him of a nature program where smaller insects used their numbers to devour an impossibly large creature. Skinny screamed a dark deep burst that expressed anger rather than pain. Gwion, Patrick, Grub, and Mark were also now completely covered by Darwinians like Skinny.

'Warriors, hold fast!' came a shout from above.

Zachary looked up and watched his father spin his staff over his head like he had in the marketplace, except this time, the staff and his father were four times bigger. Zachary knew what was coming, and within seconds, the loudest bang of all went off and a blue flash blasted down around Zachary and stripped the Darwinians from their victims, leaving the giant monsters crouching on the floor in the pulsing light of their own magical glow.

'Brothers, to arms. The next wave approaches,' called James.

Saskia and Rafi had now found the strength to also stick their heads up from their brother's chest and the three children looked around in awe from the pile of sleeping bags they were immersed in.

The next wave attacked in the same way, except this time they hit James first in an attempt to stop his protective blast that had thwarted the last attack.

Zachary recognised this as a smart move, but he was concerned as to who would watch over them if all the giants were covered. This was exactly the tactic the enemy was going for, and as the numbers built up on the giants, Zachary knew that they would be exposed.

'We have to move from here,' he said to his siblings.

'What? But Dad said to stay here,' called out Saskia above the noise.

'I know, but look. There are too many of them and we should slip away whilst they are all focussed on Dad and his friends.'

'Where will we go?' she called.

This was a good point. Zachary looked about frantically and could see thousands of abandoned tents and small cabins around him, leftovers from the other campers who had set up for the rodeo. He realised now why they had run away in such a panic.

'Let's use the tents and make our way back towards the city, where we can lose them in the buildings.'

Saskia nodded and Zachary moved off, stretching his body out on the floor in a commando crawl. He moved fast, using his knees and elbows to stay close to the ground. He stopped about ten feet away and looked behind him to give encouragement to his brother and sister. Saskia pushed Rafi off and made him head towards Zachary and she followed closely behind, covering his legs protectively.

The children covered ground quickly, and within a minute, they were outside the circle of giants and still unnoticed by anyone due to the immense battle going on overhead. They reached the nearest tent and all huddled together momentarily to check one another. Then Zachary pointed to the next tent, a couple feet away. Once away from the main attack zone, they were able to make light work of their movements, flinging themselves from one opening to another. Before long, they were reaching the edge of the campsite and could see the abandoned market channel where they had been shopping only a few hours earlier. They were about to make the last run to reach the edge when a massive fireball blew a giant gash in the tents, exposing the path ahead. The children jumped back and lay for a second in fear. They found their feet and crouched in a small red tent next to the trails of the fireball.

'There is no more cover, so we will have to make a run to the city edge,' Zachary told the others.

They all looked out the tent at the buildings on the edge of the city ahead of them.

It's too far. Someone will see us,' said Saskia and Rafi nodded in fear.

'What other choice do we have?'

Zachary stared open-mouthed at the battle they had just left behind. The other two children followed suit and all three stood in silence, watching what was now taking place. Skinny was battling a giant two-headed king cobra. He had a hand around one of its necks and the other was holding his white sword and slashing defensively against the other writhing head, as well as defending against boulders and Darwinians flying in. The snake was growing in size as they battled, and when Skinny sliced one of the heads off, two more appeared in its place.

Three jet-black dragons materialised overhead and swooped down to attack the Warriors. They were each the size of three double-decker London buses in length and were at least two buses wide, with long tails that were spiked all the way to the large bulbous end that they used to smash about in hopes of crushing the Warriors. They were breathing out long, large bursts of fire over the battle and flying about at a speed too fast for their size.

The ground shuddered with a deep, hollow boom and the three children's attention switched to the left side of the battle as they watched a giant man that looked as if he was made from stone step over the marketplace and make his way to the fighting. He was at least one hundred feet tall and dwarfed anyone and anything around him. As he got near the range of the fighting area, he swung his massive arm down onto Mark, who was destroying one of the dragons. Mark noticed the incoming arm just in time and moved out of the way. He escaped getting hit by no more than an inch.

The sound and vibration from the giant flooded through the ground and Mark was immediately in the air, flipping up high above the giant with a bright emerald-green broadsword that he drove hard into its head. The sword flashed with light and the giant's head exploded in a rain of rocks and boulders. The giant's body then disappeared into a million grains of dust. More giant booms signified the coming of three more stone giants who were all climbing over the marketplace.

Zachary tore his vision away from the battle and looked beyond where the giants had come from. He could see several figures floating in the air, swishing and throwing their limbs around as if they were fighting an invisible enemy around them. He looked back at the battle, then back at the distant figures, and waited for an explosion of light so he could get another glimpse of them. As he watched, he noticed that the movements they mimed matched the actions of the giants, snakes, and dragons in the battle.

'They are Conjurers,' he said quietly to himself.

This woke the other two from their daze.

'What did you say?' said Saskia.

'Conjurers over there—look.'

He pointed to where the figures were hanging in the air and they waited for a flash of light. A large bout of fire burst from one of the dragons, lighting up the sky so that the three children could watch them in action.

'Did you see them? Did you see what they are doing?' shouted Zachary.

'Is that what you are?' asked Rafi.

'Yes, I think so, and I think that's what they are,' replied Zachary. 'We have to help Dad.'

'How? What can we do?' asked Rafi.

'Saskia, find Dad and tell him where they are in your head.'

She frowned and looked worried.

'I'll try,' she said quietly.

She held her eyes shut tight and slowed her breathing.

'He's panicked and wants to know where we are,' she said.

'Don't tell him,' Zachary said sharply, 'in case someone is listening, like you do.'

She nodded.

'Tell him we are safe and together, but make sure you tell him about the Conjurers and where they are.'

She nodded again and closed her eyes. A few seconds passed slowly.

'He said, "Hold tight my babies, Mum will be here any second," and "Thank you". Oh, and he said, "Watch this".'

They all looked towards the battle in the distance. The giant crimson devil that was their father fell from his position in the air and landed squat on the ground. He sprang up with incredible speed, performing a graceful upward swoop to a very high peak, stalling momentarily, closing into a ball and opened into a perfect swan dive towards the location where the Conjurers were. As he flew through the air, James stretched his arms into a V-shape. He then turned and somersaulted to bounce off the boulders, a giant eagle, and even more dragons that the Conjurers threw at him as they tried desperately to prevent his approach.

James was too agile. He continued to bounce and somersault as he destroyed the assault of horrors the Conjurers placed before him. He continued on until he was upon them and cutting them down in the sky. Some tried to retreat, but he lassoed them with a bolt of energy from his staff and reined them within his reach, where he proceeded to spin the remaining two Conjurers into a whirlwind of white mist. Once it cleared, the children could see that they had been turned into stone and their screams of terror had been perfectly preserved on their faces. The stone statues fell to the ground and shattered upon impact.

James looked about and bolted back to the main fight, which was still raging. Luckily, the giants, snakes, boulders and dragons had all exploded into clouds of grey dust upon the demise of their creators.

'Let's make a run for it,' Zachary said to the others.

They all agreed and the three children took a deep breath together.

'When I count to three, we run and stick together. Ok?'

They all hugged one another tightly and steadied themselves, focussing their vision on the buildings only two hundred metres away.

'One, two, three!'

The three children bolted out from the red tent and into the open. Zachary positioned himself behind the other two and yelled encouragement.

A thud ahead stopped the children in their tracks as a figure dressed in all black landed directly in their path.

'Going somewhere?' The familiar figure stretched his mouth into a cruel smile.

'Teivel,' whispered Saskia.

'Oh, you have heard of me, how nice.' He held his walking stick up towards the sky and a beacon of light pulsed from it in a long, narrow beam.

'Get out of our way!' called Zachary in a strong voice that did not match his inner feelings.

'I don't think so, little one.' Teivel stretched this sentence out painfully slowly.

More thuds around the children made them jump as black-suited Darwinians landed, forming a circle around them. They were of varying sizes, ranging from average height for an adult to fifteen-foot giants almost as large as the Warriors, but without the bright colours or monstrous features. Each one was wearing a matching black jacket and trouser suit, a white shirt, and a black tie—the standard uniform for a Darwinian. There was one space left in the circle, which offered the children a way out back in the direction they had come and they instinctively edged towards it. All the surrounding suits were watching them with dead expressions, apart from Teivel, who watched with his cruel smirk. The children were almost at the gap, and all the while, the Darwinians held their positions. Zachary turned and shouted for the other two to run. He threw himself at the gap and ran head first into a massive Darwinian who landed with a loud thud before him. This one was the largest of them all at eighteen feet tall. He was wearing the standard uniform along with the addition of a black bowler hat.

'Hadrian Von Hellbitten, at your service,' said the giant Darwinian looking down at the children. 'I am exceptionally pleased to meet you.' He smirked.

'What are you going to do to us?' Zachary called out.

'We want to look after you and train you, what else?' he said as his face broke into a gentler smile.

Zachary frowned, not knowing how to process this response.

'This was never about harming you. This is about ensuring you survive and making sure we can work together to benefit and help mankind.'

As he spoke, Hadrian stepped forwards and shrank down to his normal size of six feet five inches and his lean build. He reached a hand out to Zachary, offering him a hand shake.

'Let us protect you and teach you to become the great Olympians we know you are. Work with us and we can give you the world—a better, more peaceful world.' His face broke into a soft smile again and he kneeled down on one knee before them and removed his hat to reveal oiled jet-black hair that had been combed perfectly into a side parting.

'We can be a perfect team. You must trust me,' he pleaded. As he looked longingly at the children, a blue half-dome suddenly appeared around them and they instantly disappeared.

Jenna hovered overhead inside a shield of her own, preventing her from being seen or heard. She turned her attention to the Warriors in the throes of battle and cast a shield over them. Each one felt her barrier envelop them and paused for breath, taking the opportunity to recharge themselves back up. Her immense power allowed the Warriors to fight with bolder and more daring moves, all the while knowing that if something got through their guard, it would have to be pretty big to get through Jenna's shield.

The battle quickly turned in the Warriors' favour and they started to make lighter work of the attacking Darwinians. Sensing this, the masses began to retreat, offering dangerous space to James and the others that they enveloped immediately, swallowing up ground and punishing the Darwinians at every step.

As Hadrian watched, his face contorted into a grimace and he tore his gaze from the battle he was now losing back to where the children had disappeared. His body flashed from the inside with light and he grew to his giant self in seconds and screamed:

'Nooo! Aaah!'

The other Darwinians in the circle cowered and backed away. The three children were invisible to them, but they were in the centre of the circle, crouched low. They held their hands over their ears upon hearing such a harsh, loud scream.

Hadrian hulked his mass over the spot where the children had disappeared.

'You are still here, aren't you? I can feel your presence.'

He walked forwards and his giant strides came down on the children. They scrambled out the way, not knowing if their actions would make them visible, but they remained hidden. Unfortunately, Rafi was separated from his two older siblings and they sat on opposite sides of the raging giant, who was stomping around, trying to find a sign of the children. Jenna was screaming for James to come telepathically and he heard every word of it. He was quickly approaching and was closely followed by the other Warriors. Hadrian looked up and watched him draw near. James was over one hundred metres away, but he stared directly into Hadrian's eyes as he flipped, smashed, and powered his way forwards like an American football player running through a crowd of children.

Hadrian sized himself up and placed the fingers of his right hand delicately into the inside sleeve of his left arm, removing a long, sleek black wand. He raised it high above his head like a conductor about to begin directing an orchestra and waited for the imminent attack. The other Darwinians in the circle backed even further away and the three children in the centre stood up and watched.

At over thirty metres away, James leapt head first directly at Hadrian. James was holding his staff with both hands over his head, ready to swing down upon his victim like a monstrous red executioner.

James was moments away from striking and Hadrian braced himself for action. He was not afraid, he had been in many battles before. He had even won against bigger and more dangerous enemies. It was at this moment that Jenna realised she had been distracted in watching the horror of the situation and that James knew nothing of the children's whereabouts.

'*They are behind him!*' she screamed in her head.

James went wide-eyed, panicked, and twisted in the air, flying past Hadrian and into a commando roll on the floor to his left. Hadrian had not expected this and the powerful burst from his wand streamed past where James had just been. James looked about in a panic, silently asking Jenna where the children were. She waved her hand down high above them and they appeared to James alone. His gaze fixed on Rafi, who stood beyond Hadrian, and then on the two children now between him and his enemy. He looked up to see a look of realisation reach Hadrian's face and this struck terror into his heart. He had given the children's positions away through his fear and panic. Hadrian stretched his face into a cruel smile and straightened his body, raising his hand to strike with his wand at the empty space before him.

'Don't do it, please!' James pleaded.

There was a pause that lasted an eternity and then Hadrian's wand glowed brightly at the tip.

James flung himself in-front of the children as Hadrian knew he would and the blast hit him full in the chest. It was a move that would have killed anyone that was shielded by a lesser protector, but Jenna's strength held fast. James flew back and crashed at the feet of the two older children, sending them flying backwards and landing harshly on the hard ground.

Zachary picked himself up slowly and looked over at his sister. His eyes flew open in shock as she was glowing bright white and getting brighter by the second. He looked over at his father and Hadrian, who had both started backing off. James was wearing a look of terror on his face. Zachary felt a strong wind blowing through his insides, and all at once he felt as light as a feather. He looked down at the ground to see it moving slowly away. Then he looked over at Saskia and saw that she was crying, glowing as bright as the Sun from inside and also floating up slowly in a gust of air. Zachary reached a hand out to her and could see that his own hand was also glowing bright white. He withdrew it in shock and looked at his pulsing, white hands in awe.

Jenna braced herself for what she knew was to come next. She felt the two explosions rise up beneath her and pushed all her energy through her necklace to her loved ones below. Then the world went dark, and she fell from the sky in a rush of wind.

Chapter 10: The Darkness

The darkness seemed infinite. The silence was deafening. What was this existence? There was a muffled sound, like a voice talking into a pillow. It was a man's voice speaking slowly and calmly. Another voice, a woman's voice, answered in a higher tone: 'What are they saying? Who are they? Where am I? Where are my babies? My babies!'

Jenna wrestled with consciousness for the next two minutes as her internal struggle to awaken and protect her children fought against her body's need to recover from the explosions.

She moaned as her desperation peaked. The voices stopped. Silence and darkness followed.

The muffled voices were back, and louder than before.

'What are they saying?' she thought. *'Who are they?'*

Jenna struggled to say something.

'Help me,' she called.

From somewhere outside her body came a moan and the voices stopped again.

'No, don't go! Don't leave me,' she called. 'Please, help me!' she called out in a moan.

'Ow.' Something hurt.

What hurt? She pondered where the pain was located. It was her arm. Something was pinching her arm really hard—a sharp pain. Jenna suddenly felt conscious of the fact that she had a body. Up until now, she had been a voice, a life floating in the darkness. The pain gave her back a physical presence. The voices came back for a moment and then they changed to be gently softer, as if the volume were being turned down, slowly. Finally, they went into the darkness again.

A touch, softness against her skin. '*Something touched me*', she thought. The volume was being turned up, and the voices were back. They were louder this time and she struggled to hear.

'*Don't speak, Jenna,*' she thought, '*just listen.*'

The voices were just out of reach. They were almost audible but never quite there. Suddenly, there was a word, an audible word, in the darkness. The woman said two words and the second word was definitely 'drugs'. Her tone was anxious and she was not happy with what the man was saying.

They were arguing, but not shouting. They were debating. She was getting excited. More words!

'This is not why I became a nurse!' she said, clearly irritated.

'*A nurse!*' thought Jenna, '*I need a nurse.*'

'Nurse!' she called out and her external body actually said this word, clearly and strenuously this time. A long silence followed.

'Nurse!' called Jenna.

'Do it now!' the man said firmly and Jenna heard this with complete clarity.

'*Do what now?*' she thought. '*Ow.*' The pain in her arm returned and the volume was slowly being turned down again.

'*An injection,*' she thought. '*Drugs! I am in trouble,*' she realised.

She slowly drifted away from consciousness. Her last thought before she lost her battle once more was that of a protection shield against the drugs. She said it over and over again in her head and felt the power flow through her before she lost her body to the darkness once more.

The voices were back, but this time, they were different. They were calm and patient, with an air of kindness about them. The woman was there and then the man was talking again. She felt the new presence before he spoke, a strong presence with immense power and familiarity.

'*Is it James,*' she thought.

Jenna was too afraid to speak in case they drugged her again. James would not allow her to be drugged, so she knew it was not him.

'She's coming around,' said the woman.

A shard of light, a blinding beam, came through the crack in her eyelids.

'Pull the blinds please, nurse,' said the new voice.

The light became bearable and Jenna dared to open her other eye. She struggled to focus, and desperation made her cry out once again.

'Please try to relax, Jenna. You are safe and you are well. Please relax and allow yourself to wake up slowly.'

'My children,' she breathed.

'They are safe,' came the man's voice and she knew it was true. She could feel their presence, but did not allow herself to believe her feelings. A tear rolled down her cheek.

'Please, come around slowly, Jenna.'

Her focus was improving by the second and she was beginning to see shadows and the first signs of colour. She could make out the outlines of the three people standing around her bed. Two people were on the right and one was on the left. The room was white and had pictures on the wall painted in soft colours. The people were coming into view and she could see the nurse smiling at her, then glancing up above her head.

'*She is looking at monitors,*' thought Jenna. '*I am in a hospital.*'

Jenna looked at the man next to her in the white coat with a stethoscope around his neck.

'*He's a doctor,*' she thought.

'Welcome back, Jenna,' he said. 'You gave us all quite a scare.'

Jenna smiled back at him and recognised his voice as the man arguing with the nurse.

'Welcome back, Jenna,' came the new voice.

She looked over.

'You? How . . . what happened? Why have you brought me here, Hadrian?' she said, becoming agitated.

'Now, now, Jenna, stay calm. You are perfectly safe. We are here to help.'

'Help yourself, perhaps.'

'Tut, tut, you have been around that angry husband of yours for too long. We are the good guys. Why else would we have saved your life and look after your children until you came around?' he asked.

Jenna knew she was being drugged. She had realised this and had protected herself from whatever it was they had been giving her, but they did not know this. This fact was her only advantage, she thought.

'I want to see my children.'

'Of course, you do. We will bring them to see you.'

'I want to see them now!' she said with the renewed strength that was growing by the second.

'You have just woken from a long, deep, sleep. I think a little rest is in order.'

'How long have I been out?' she asked the nurse sternly.

The nursed glanced at Hadrian, who nodded.

'*He controls everything,*' she thought, '*and everyone.*'

'A little over eight weeks,' said the nurse weakly as she reached out and placed her hand gently on Jenna's.

'*How much of that time was drug-induced?*' Jenna wondered. Jenna thought about this for a moment. 'And James? And the Warriors?' she looked Hadrian straight in his eyes.

He sighed.

'I'm afraid it's not good news.' He shifted uncomfortably in his seat. 'They did not survive the blasts. You only had strength to protect yourself and the children.'

Jenna's eyes filled with tears and they rolled down her face.

'But you survived! You were there.'

'I only survived because I was within the circle of protection you cast over your children when the blasts went off. Everyone else within the campsite was killed immediately.'

Jenna looked beyond the room and stretched her feelings, searching for James, but there was nothing, not even a glimmer of his existence. He was simply not there.

'You managed to save the city and everyone in it,' Hadrian continued. 'The blasts would have wiped the valley and a large part of Peru from existence. Somehow, you managed to stem the blast to a containment area of approximately two hundred metres, which is quite remarkable to say the least.'

'It was not enough,' she retorted.

'It was enough to save your children.'

'But I didn't save them. You have them now.'

'We are not the enemy Jenna,' Hadrian pleaded.

'What kind of friend attacks my children with an army?'

'I can understand how that must look, but we were there for the children. It was imperative that we got to them before the League found them. The League wants to train your children to rule the world under their tyranny. Imagine a world ruled by the

Olympians again! The League has no respect for humankind or our brothers and sisters. We had to find them first and teach them to rule with compassion and love for all.'

'Then why not ask? Why not come to us?'

'Your husband and his friends would never have allowed that. They all feared us and would have protected the children from us to their dying breaths.'

He stopped, realising he had been insensitive, given that they had indeed given their last breaths. An uncomfortable silence followed.

'I want to see my children,' Jenna repeated.

'Soon,' said Hadrian in a relaxed voice.

'Now!' Jenna said firmly, ripping the drip from her arm and moving to stand.

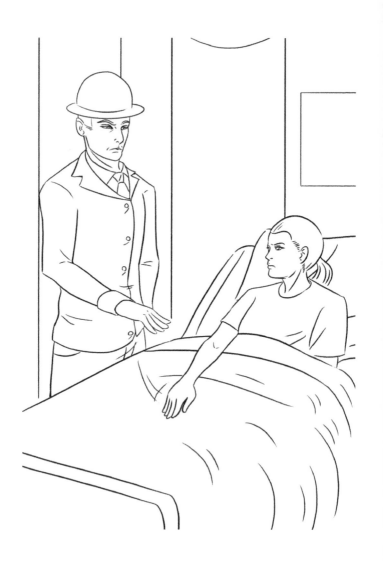

'Ok, ok, please, stay in bed and I will have them brought to you now.'

Hadrian nodded to the doctor, who immediately left the room.

'So, what now?' asked Jenna? 'Are we your prisoners?'

'For now, yes. But we are under no illusions. Your children's powers will soon supersede ours. We will give them the best education money can buy. They will learn from the greatest minds and scholars of our time, one on one. We will put everything we can into them, and in time, the world will benefit from this investment.'

Jenna raised an eyebrow.

'Not such a bad thought,' Hadrian continued.

'And what is this place? A hospital?'

'This is one of hundreds of state-of-the-art facilities built and maintained by Darwinian Global. You are in the hospital wing, which is the envy of the most prestigious and expensive hospitals in the world. Everything we do, we strive to be the best at. This hospital, for example, is the centre of excellence in several fields, like stem cell and degenerative condition research. We help thousands of people every day.

'The education department, which your children are being taught in as we speak, has results beyond any other school and is only matched by similar facilities we have in other countries. The *pièce de résistance* is our science and magic wing, the focal point of the most powerful countries and people in the world. Within its walls, we teach and train wizards and those exceptionally fortunate non-wizards on how to combine science and magic to become powerful peacekeepers, following the strict guidelines of those elected to power.'

'Who polices the policemen?' Jenna mumbled.

'What?' Hadrian replied tersely.

'Where am I?' asked Jenna, diverting Hadrian's attention from an obvious sore point.

'The greatest city of them all: London.'

'And the Prime Minister, the elected power, has approved keeping us prisoners, has he?'

'For the moment, yes. I simply showed him photos of ground zero in Peru. The conversation didn't last much longer than that, I'm afraid.'

'Mummmmy!' came the scream from the doorway.

Zachary, Saskia, and Rafi came charging in and cuddled as closely as they could to their mother.

Chapter 11: A Brave New World

'Tell me everything. What have I missed?' Jenna asked her children.

'This place is awesome!' cried Zachary. 'It's like a spaceship. We can have almost anything to eat, we don't have to tidy up, school is a breeze, and they are teaching us magic!'

Hadrian stood, leaning against the far wall, and smiled at the children's enthusiasm.

'Whoa, slow down tiger,' Jenna interrupted. 'Anything you want to eat?'

'Well, almost, but its balanced meals. It's free and we don't have to clear up.' He smiled.

'You like the school here?' Jenna asked Saskia.

'Yes!' she cried. 'My teachers really like me, and I have made friends already with some of the other girls in my class.'

'That sounds great, baby girl. How about you, my lovely little man?' she asked Rafi next.

He looked pale, and after initially seeing his mother, he seemed sad.

'Where is my daddy? They said he was with you and that we could see him soon,' he said quietly.

The children's excitement faded and they looked at their mother expectantly.

'I thought it was better coming from you. I think it's best for me to leave you alone,' said Hadrian and he left the room.

'I'm so pleased to see you safe, my babies,' said Jenna, stalling the horror of what she had to say next.

'He's gone, isn't he?' said Zachary. 'I knew they were lying.'

Jenna looked at her children and simply nodded. They all came closer and hugged her tightly.

'Will you die soon?' asked Rafi.

'No darling, I will not leave you. I am here always,' she said with tears streaming down her face.

Jenna got up, dressed, and argued with Hadrian about moving into the children's dormitory. He conceded on the grounds that they had just lost their father and that she would not co-operate otherwise. A bright and modern apartment was prepared and given to her. It was situated directly next door to where the children and several others were staying in a similar-styled dormitory that housed eight children in total.

She took her time going round the dorm and paid attention to each of her children's sleeping areas, chatting with them a bit and giving them some kind of normality in the otherwise chaotic life they have been living over the past few weeks. She met the dorm nanny, Renee, a pretty blonde woman with cold blue eyes and a harsh demeanour. Jenna realised she had taken Renee's room through her insistence that she be near the children and put her harshness down to her recent eviction.

'My element is redwood, like Dad's,' said Zachary.

His face sunk as he remembered there was no Daddy anymore.

'Mine is glass,' said Saskia, distracting him, 'like yours, Mummy.'

'And what is yours, my littlest wizard?' Jenna asked Rafi. He looked paler than before and he was now breathing heavily.

'It's water, Mummy. Watch this.'

Rafi waved his hand towards the glass of water by his bed, and all at once, the water inside floated up in several bubbles and then joined to make one large bubble that he moved over closer to his hand. As it wobbled in the air, he waved his little hand over it and it stretched out to become a long thin wand shape. He opened his palm flat underneath it and the wand went white as it froze and fell into his hand.

'I can make a wand anywhere,' he said and smiled weakly.

'That's amazing!' said Jenna.

'I love it when he does that,' said Zachary.

'Do you know your other elements yet? You know, the one that takes power from you?' asked Jenna.

The children all shook their heads.

'Good, you are better off not knowing.'

'Bedtime!' called Renee.

All the children milling around the dormitory groaned and stopped playing their computer games or reading books and started getting ready for bed. Jenna helped her children and talked to some of the others as she did this. The other children were extremely well-behaved. She met twins called Michael and Caroline and then a tiny polite girl called Bluebell. She presumed these children were so polite due to their parent's high position in society, which had allowed them to get into this school.

Jenna got Renee's attention and asked for a quiet word with her. They moved to the games room, located off the main dorm.

'Rafi is unwell. We need to call a doctor,' said Jenna.

'He is tired and pale, but that's perfectly normal when someone so young first uses their powers,' replied Renee.

'No, it's more than that,' Jenna replied.

'He simply needs rest. Besides, all the doctors have gone home.'

'Well, get one back—he's unwell, I tell you.'

'How about this? If he is still unwell in the morning, we will call a doctor first thing.'

Jenna agreed, but was not happy and they re-entered the dorm as the children were preparing for bed. Some were brushing their teeth and others were changing into bedclothes or washing their faces in the big bathroom off from the main dormitory where the beds were. The ceiling-to-floor window at the end of the room that let in vast amounts of light was being closed off by an electric blind. Jenna had not really looked out of it, but as the blind was going down she noticed the spectacular view of London beneath them and realised the vastness of the building they were in as the dormitory was so high up. She guessed they were around sixty floors up.

'That will not do!' Renee snapped at a child, awakening Jenna from her daze. She was heading to Saskia's bed, where Rafi had cuddled up to his sister and was hanging on.

'Please, Renee, let me sleep here,' Rafi was saying and gripping tightly to Saskia, who was hanging on to him just as tightly.

'No. It is not allowed for children to share beds,' she replied harshly.

'Why not!' Jenna pitched in.

'We look after over two thousand children in this facility alone. Imagine how it would be if we did not have hard rules to manage them.'

'I understand and it's a good point,' Jenna conceded. She moved in close to Renee and whispered, 'They have just lost their father and their home in the space of a few weeks, plus Rafi is unwell. Please, let them, just this once.'

'No, it is not allowed,' Renee replied loudly in Jenna's face and proceeded to turn and pull them apart. The children

164

tensed for a fight and Zachary looked on at Renee with hatred, his hand playing with his wand by his side. He wondered if he should take matters into his own hands.

'Stop!' Jenna called out and everyone froze. 'Don't touch my children!' she snarled. 'I'll do it, if it must be done.'

Jenna bent down and whispered to her two smallest children, then prised Rafi from his sister, placing him into his own bed. She noticed that Renee must have pressed a panic button as a shadow in the doorway alerted Jenna to a guard that had been called and he was now backing away at a nod from Renee. Jenna realised immediately that this reaction was excessive for a simple sleeping rule and made a mental note to ponder it later, when the children were asleep.

She tucked them in and sang to the whole dorm of children, which they thoroughly enjoyed, having been too long without a mother's love. She kissed all of them in turn and then sat on a chair near the window and opened it just enough to take in the view again, sitting near her children in the darkness until they slept.

Jenna set herself up by the window for a long stay, determined to wait until her body ached for sleep. She pulled over a stool for her feet and a small table for her glass of water. She relaxed into the big white leather chair and reclined, whilst looking out over sleepy London.

By ten thirty, all the children were fast asleep. Jenna frowned at Rafi's heavy breath and paleness, and then he began to moan in his sleep and a strong temperature came on, along with a nosebleed. Jenna looked anxiously around the room for new sheets, but the best she could do was put a towel under his head where the blood had fallen. She knelt by his bed and stroked his head for many hours.

At two a.m., she woke up, still kneeling next to Rafi. She had placed her head by his. He looked terrible, she thought, and she would insist on seeing a doctor at first light. Saskia moaned quickly and quietly in the bed next door and she realised it was this that had woken her. Jenna got to her feet slowly because kneeling for such a long time had made them ache. Jenna moved over to where Saskia was, listening as she moaned again while sleeping. She knelt down next to her and it was now Saskia's turn to be stroked by her mother. She must have been having a bad dream, thought Jenna, as the moans seemed rhythmic and came at roughly the same interval of every thirty seconds.

'Shhh, hush, my baby. It's ok,' whispered Jenna.

That was when she saw it. No one else would have or could have noticed this, but Saskia had made her awake and alert, and there it was right in front of her eyes. With every rhythmic moan Saskia gave, her glass of water on the side table rippled ever so slightly. It was almost invisible, as if someone had tapped the table and caused a minute vibration to run through the surface of the water. Jenna watched for a minute, and there it was again, a moan from Saskia and the matching ripple through the glass. Jenna knew the ripple came from a low-level vibration coming through the building. Such a thing would normally be caused by the London tube lines, but this was not that. This was a near invisible vibration running through the building, one that would cause her daughter's inner feelings to stir.

Jenna closed her eyes and waited for the next vibration. She focussed on the water, channelling her thoughts through the molecules, feeling the glass around them and the table beneath. She stretched her senses through these objects down to the depths of the building and still further. Jenna stretched and focussed, causing a frown to mar her face as she held her eyes closed tight. Her body ached for the source and she felt as though she was becoming part of the building.

'Boom!' and there it was. Jenna was so deeply focussed in through the glass, leaving behind only the slightest sense of Saskia to alert her to the timing, that the slight vibration hit her like a train as it ran through the building that she had become. She jumped back and landed splayed out on her back, exhausted and frightened. Jenna's eyes flew open and it was at that moment that she realised what it was. It was the noise of a trapped ghost, it was the noise of desperation, and it was the noise of an imprisoned Warrior: it was James.

Chapter 12: Trapped

'*Liars! I knew I couldn't trust them. James is alive, and he's in pain. I must get to him. Together, we can get out of here. I need to free him and let him destroy them,*' thought Jenna.

'*What else has he lied about? This school? My children?*' She looked around at the other sleeping children and wondered who they were. Perhaps they were just actors and actresses staging a performance. She looked at her own babies and at her pale, sick littlest one.

'*The bed!*'

Jenna flew up and made her way over to Rafi.

'*Why the big fuss about this bed? Why must he sleep in it? Why call the guard when he threatened not to? Don't be obvious, Jenna. Don't let them see.*'

She knelt next to Rafi, placed her hand on his forehead, and immediately felt him burning up. She wanted to cry, but she knew doing this would only be a weakness and she needed her strength and cunning.

As she stroked Rafi's head, she leaned over him and kissed his face, staying in this position of a mother's smothering love whilst shielding her other hand from view as it crawled around the bed, searching for something out of place. She searched for many minutes and found nothing. Frustration hit her and she moved around to his other side and completed the same manoeuvre. Again, she found nothing. She stood and ran her hands through her thick hair and noticed she was breathing heavily.

'*Calm down, Jenna. Breathe. If you calm down, the solution will present itself.*'

She knelt next to Rafi again and watched his shallow, slow breathing. She mimicked his breaths and began to calm herself down. She breathed slowly and focussed on Rafi, and when she felt calm and relaxed, she leaned in once more, but instead of moving her hand around the bed and looking for something to touch that was out of place, she slipped her hand under the mattress between Rafi's head and the base of the bed, just letting it rest there. Jenna closed her eyes once more and searched with her feelings this time and felt her son above and below her hand.

'What! I feel Rafi above and below my hand,' she thought. 'How is this possible?'

She placed her hand lower down on the bed and there she felt more of Rafi under the bed than above it.

'How is this possible? What are they doing to him? This bed is killing him.'

She stood and walked over to Saskia, cuddling closely to the sleeping eight-year-old. Once again, she slipped her hand under the mattress and focussed. Nothing, she felt nothing underneath her bed. Jenna stood and walked over to Zachary and performed the same manoeuvre. Nothing again. She stood and walked over to the chair by the window and perched on the edge of the seat.

Jenna sat for two and half minutes, and by the end of that time, she had devised a risky and dangerous plan that put her and her children in great danger, but she knew that they were already in great danger.

She looked at Saskia and sent a message over to her head.

'Sassy, Sassy, wake up, my princess. Sassy, my baby girl, wake up, my darling, I need your help.'

Saskia slowly came too and rubbed her eyes.

Jenna walked over to Saskia and held her close. She laid her back down and whispered in her ear. Saskia nodded, closed her eyes, and rested. Jenna walked back over to the chair and focussed on Zachary.

'Zacky, Zacky, wake up, my baby boy. Zacky, please wake up, I need your help.'

Zachary stayed in his sleeping position, but his eyes popped open.

'Five more minutes,' he moaned, thinking it was school time.

Jenna walked to his side and snuggled with him. She whispered in his ear and he nodded and closed his eyes.

Jenna stood and walked to the door that led to her bedroom off the main dormitory. She looked back at her children and then went into the bedroom, closing the door behind her. She lay down on the bed, closed her eyes, and waited for ten anxious minutes.

'Ahhh!' came Saskia's scream in the other room. 'Give me back my Chummy! Give it back, give it back!'

Saskia was going hysterical and Jenna had to fight herself from getting up and going to her.

'What's going on in here?' came Renee's cold voice.

'He took my Chummy and I want it back!' Saskia screamed.

'I don't have it! She's mad. She hit my face and scratched me!' a boy called out.

Jenna held the small pink teddy bear that Saskia called 'Chummy' tight in her hands in the other room and felt pride at how strong her daughter was and how scared she must be.

'Give her back her Chummy!' came Zachary's voice, strong and determined.

'Everybody settle down and get into your beds.'

'No! I will not settle down until he gives me my Chummy back!' screamed Saskia with unusual venom.

'I don't have it, I tell you.'

'I saw you looking at it, and now it's gone. Give it back now!' she screamed again.

Saskia charged at the little boy, who ran across the room away from her. Renee grabbed her arm.

'Let go of my sister!' cried Zachary as he leapt on Renee's back and pulled her hair hard.

'Ahhh! Get off!' she screamed.

Jenna burst in through the door.

'What on Earth is going on here?' she called out.

Renee let go of Saskia and she charged after the terrified boy, who ran to the door of the dormitory to find it locked and turned to see a screaming Saskia running at him. He panicked and ran round the room and through Jenna's open door. Saskia ran in after him and a loud explosion followed.

'Good gracious!' screamed Renee.

Smoked bellowed out of Jenna's room and the terrified boy ran out with black stuff all over his face.

'She's mad! Help me—she's crazy!' he screamed.

'Aaahhh! Give me back Chummy!' Saskia kept screaming after him.

'Stop immediately!' screeched Renee and she held up her wand, which was bright green and shiny.

'Don't you dare.' Jenna held out her necklace, pointing it at Renee, who froze with fear.

Another explosion went off behind Renee at the door of the dormitory. This time, the explosion was powerful enough to blow the door away completely, exposing the corridor outside.

The terrified boy crouched on the floor next to the door. Jenna marvelled at how accurate her daughter's aim was, and that she had blown the door away without hurting anyone. The boy noticed the hole and charged through it, closely followed by the still screaming, wild Saskia, with her wand held high in an attack position.

'Come back this instant!' screamed Renee, now in complete shock.

'Don't just stand there, you idiot! Let's go after her before she kills him!' Jenna yelled in Renee's face.

The two women charged out, followed by all the children in the dormitory. More explosions could be heard down the hall.

Zachary crept out from the smoke in Jenna's room and stayed still for a second. He jumped when he saw several guards in the standard-issue black suit and white shirt run past. He knew he only had a few minutes, so he jumped to his task.

He pulled on his bed to bring it out to the centre of the room. It was extremely heavy and he was unsure about whether he could push it back, but he knew failure was not an option and he focussed all his strength on pulling it. It was simply too heavy and he was not big enough. He stood over it and looked at his sick little brother, who lay unconscious and oblivious to the chaos that just took place.

Then Zachary brightened and took out his wand. He raised it high and focussed on pulling the bed out, channelling his strength. The bed glided out with such speed that it took him by surprise and he sharpened the angle of his wand so that it came to an abrupt stop. He twisted his wand in the air and the mattress floated up, leaving the bare base. He stared down at the sight before him with curiosity. The bed stand was made of metal, but hidden from view was a hollow square rectangle that stretched to the edges of the bed frame and had a glass top that was hinged at one side, he presumed, so that it could be opened. Beneath the glass layer were hundreds of tiny glass test tubes, all being held in their own tiny holes. There were hundreds of them in neat little rows that resembled little soldiers in a tiny march. He bent down and looked at the test tubes and could see different samples in each of them of a variety of colours and textures, and no two were the same. He paused and took a mental image of them as his mother had asked and then gently placed the mattress back down as he had found it.

He turned his attention to his little brother and walked over to his small sleeping body. Zachary picked him up with ease and placed him neatly in his own bed. He then used his power to swiftly and easily swap the beds' positions around, so that Rafi was tucked up neatly in Zachary's bed. Zachary took care to make sure that Rafi was still in the position he was in when everyone had left. Then Zachary smiled to himself and went to hide back in Jenna's room until everyone returned. It had quietened down outside now and he knew they would be back any second. He paused at the entrance to his mother's room and turned to look at Rafi's bed. He held his wand high and the mattress floated up to reveal the same base as before except now the room lit up with a bright blue glow coming from the base of the bed.

Zachary's eyebrows rose in surprise and he paused in awe. He bent over and squinted at the brightness of the glow coming from the hundreds of tiny test tubes. Inside each one was a small blue rock glowing with immense power. Zachary reeled at the thought that hit him like a truck. This was Rafael's second element, the one that takes power. The Darwinians had somehow figured out what it was and were draining his little brother of his power, making him weak and sick. Zachary made the connection to his own bed and realised they were testing elements on him one night at a time and probably on his sister, too. A noise from outside broke his thoughts and he placed the mattress down with speed, tucked both beds in neatly, ran back to his mother's room, and waited with fear and anger running through his veins.

Jenna re-entered the dormitory with Saskia wrapped around her, head buried in her mother's neck. She held her Chummy between her body and her mother's and looked as if she was very happy to have it back. Jenna looked around for Zachary and saw his timid face in her bedroom. He nodded, letting her know the task was done and she relaxed a little. The rest of the children followed quietly, talking about the excitement, and then entered Renee. She wore a steely expression and half of her face was black. She was holding the hand of a very frightened-looking boy covered in dirt.

'I didn't take it! I didn't. I don't know where it came from, but I didn't. I didn't take it,' he muttered.

The children were all settled down in their beds and two guards were put around the hole where the door use to be.

'I'll need a new room,' Jenna told Renee.

'One has been arranged next to mine just down the hall,' she replied without looking.

'Right everyone, sleep!' called out Renee and she left the room quickly.

Jenna made sure all the children were settled and sung two more lullabies. She knew that they might be a part of a dangerous plot against her, but they were still children and she cared for them in the absence of their mother. She made her way round to Zachary and whispered in his ear.

'Well done, baby boy. You're so brave.'

'I love you, Mum,' he replied. She got up to leave, but he held onto her hand. 'Wait,' he whispered loudly.

Zachary held her close and shut his eyes. He focussed on the image of the tiny test tubes under his bed and concentrated on them so he could see it clearly in his mind. Then he pushed the photo with all his might to his mother and knew that she had received them by her sharp intake of breath.

'*That was under my bed and is now under Rafi*,' he said in his head to her.

'*Oh my goodness, they are testing you.*'

'I know.'

He focused now on the image under Rafi's bed and could see the blue glowing rocks in the test tubes clearly in his head. He then pushed the image to his mother.

'Oh G-d, that is why he's sick! They were draining him of his power to use it for themselves.'

'Won't he be ok now that we have moved him?'

'Yes, but he will need time to heal and they will be sure to put it back once they discover the switch.'

Jenna internally feared what they would do once they discovered the truth.

'Well done again! Now get some sleep,' she whispered.

She walked over to Saskia and snuggled with her.

'Well done, my little fire dragon,' she said to Saskia in her head.

'Thank you, Mummy. I knew we could do it.'

'You did it, baby, and I'm so proud.'

Saskia smiled to herself.

'There is one last thing I need you to do,' Jenna continued.

Saskia lifted her head off the pillow and looked into her mother's eyes.

'I need you to help Rafi. I need you to heal him.'

'I tried, Mummy, I tried so hard, but it didn't work.'

'I think tonight it will,' Jenna said and smiled back.

She picked up Saskia and carried her to Rafi's bed, placing her down on the floor next to his head. Saskia reached out her little hand and gripped her wand tightly. She gently placed the tip on Rafi's forehead and Jenna knelt in behind her, wrapping her arms around the little girl and placing her hand on Saskia's.

'Focus, little one. You are stronger than you know.'

Saskia shut her eyes and felt her power flowing through her. She let it build up in her wand hand as she was taught and paused to feel it swell within her fist. She closed her eyes tightly and Jenna felt her tense up.

'Relax,' she whispered in her ear. 'Relax and enjoy your power. It should not be a struggle or painful. It should slip from you with ease and joy. Open your eyes, Saskia, and push out your power.'

Saskia relaxed and let out a deep breath. She opened her eyes and allowed the energy in her fist to flow out through her wand. Instantly, Rafi took in a deep breath and groaned. Colour rushed back into his face and his shallow breathing changed into the strong rhythmic breath of someone in a deep sleep. His hair thickened as the sweat dried out and a gentle smile stretched across his little mouth. Saskia lifted her wand from his head and Jenna reached over her to feel his temperature. Saskia turned with a smile to see Jenna with tears running down her face.

'You're so clever—so clever! Thank you, Sassy, thank you.'

The two cuddled for a minute and only pulled apart when they noticed Rafi sitting upright.

'I'm hungry. Can I have cereal?' he asked.

Mother and daughter looked at each other and giggled. Jenna tucked Saskia into bed and found some cookies and milk in the dormitory kitchen. She watched Rafi eat them whilst stroking his head. She tucked him in and then headed out the dormitory to her new room.

'*Phase one complete,*' she thought. '*Time for phase two.*'

Chapter 13: Phase Two

Jenna stood before the door to her room and took a deep breath. She was going into the belly of the beast, walking head first into danger. She closed her eyes and let her breath out slowly. As she expelled the air from her lungs, she cloaked herself from sight and sound. She teleported through the door quickly and walked down the glossy pure white hall filled with doors that housed little glass signs in the middle indicating what was inside, but no windows. As with most buildings, the lifts were located at the centre of the structure, where the solid reinforced-concrete surrounds helped support the skeleton of the tower. Jenna reached the block of twelve lift shafts and was about to press the button.

'How would this look to the security guards?' she pondered. *'They will have cameras in each lift and monitors telling them when they are in use. A solitary lift being used at two a.m. with no one in it will certainly cause suspicion.'*

Jenna knew what she must do, but it was something she did not like and was something most Protectors were not capable of, but she was. She had to cloak herself even deeper and with more power. She could not simply transport herself to the depths of the building for she did not know where that was or how deep the building went. She had to become what was referred to in the wizarding world as a 'whisper'. Only the most powerful Protectors were able to do this and it was something revered throughout the entire wizarding community. It was the ability to pass through solid objects, to travel unseen, unheard, and untouched. Jenna clenched her fists, tensed up, took a deep breath, and then remembered her own words to her daughter only thirty minutes ago.

'Relax, Jenna. It does not have to be a struggle. It should be something wonderful and even enjoyable—just relax,' she thought to herself.

Jenna breathed slowly and concentrated. She felt her power run through her body and build up in the necklace she had wrapped around her wrist. Her body lightened and floated up two inches off the ground towards the thick steel doors of the lift. Her eyes opened and she felt the fear of seeing inside the object she was about to pass through. Her hands hit the doors and sparks flew off from the contact as the magic fought against science to let her pass. She pushed harder and more sparks flew off. She knew nothing about the outwards visibility of these sparks and pushed the thought aside. Instead, she clenched her teeth and felt the coldness of the doors on her face. This was always how it was. Whenever she attempted this task, she almost resigned herself to failure by simply thinking she was not strong enough.

'Stretch your power and remember what Nellie said: it has no upper limit. Relax and stretch yourself. James needs you. He's trapped, and you must help him,' came the voice in her head.

Jenna floated inches above the floor in front of the lift doors and reached for more and more power. She greedily accepted it and still pulled internally for more. Her arms and legs filled with heat and still she reached for more. Her whole body trembled with the amount of power she was building up, and now, her torso burned inside. It felt as though her hands were glowing white hot. She backed away from the door and opened her eyes. She could see light everywhere and wondered momentarily where it was coming from. Then she looked at her hands and saw that they were glowing bright white, as were her arms and legs. She floated up gently and wondered what was happening, and then she realised she had seen this event only a few weeks ago. Jenna had watched the same thing happen to Saskia and Zachary. This was her Dawn.

'*It can't be. I am a fully developed wizard,*' she thought. '*I know my element and I have my power. How can this be?*'

She felt afraid of what was happening and could feel the tremor of the explosion and wind rushing through her, much in the same way Saskia had described in her experience.

'*How is this possible? I had my Dawn when I was a child, that's what my mother told me. I remember waking up in bed after it happened, but I don't remember it happening.*' Jenna fought for deeper memories. '*No, I don't remember it happening. I only remember my parents saying it had, so this must be it. They must have lied. Why would they lie? What were they protecting me from? Protection—they were protecting me by lying. Why else would they have done so? But what were they protecting me from? What am I that they needed to lie and protect me from the wizarding world?*'

Jenna reasoned with herself for an answer, blocking out the power surging through her body, and all at once, it became clear.

'*I am an Olympian!*'

She knew it to be true the moment she realised it. She had never Dawned. Her family had faked her Dawn to protect her from what her children were now facing. Now, she was here about to explode with the might of a fully grown woman already with great power. Jenna accepted this with ease and allowed her body to fully absorb the immense energy currently flowing through her. She did not fight it, nor did she tense up. The power grew ever more and Jenna accepted it all. She calmly and willingly reached for more. She wanted more, and the turbulence around her grew. She pushed the power to her shield and felt it grow and pulse. The outside world saw nothing, not a glimmer or noise could be seen or heard.

In Jenna's bubble, it were as if a jet engine was being run at full throttle and the wind and light were like the centre of a nuclear bomb, getting louder and pulsing with more energy by the second. Inside, Jenna beckoned for more and more power and she could hear a whining noise building up to a higher pitch, like the screaming of an engine at full throttle—and still she reached for more. The shield around her grew ever thicker and contained every extremity of the chaos within. Then all at once she reached the ceiling, the roof of her power. It seemed as though she had travelled to the upper atmosphere of Earth and beyond, but she knew she could go no further.

The explosion came as she reached her limit and she could feel the power being expelled from her body into the shield around her, but she did not fall or falter. Jenna held strong and used the extreme power within to hold her shield tight. A tiny pop and a flicker of piecing light could be seen by the outside world for only a second. The security monitors and electricity all around the building flickered for that one moment and then it was contained, thereafter, nothing more was seen. The guards stationed all over the facility thought nothing of the power glitch in a big building in Central London and continued on with their mundane tasks.

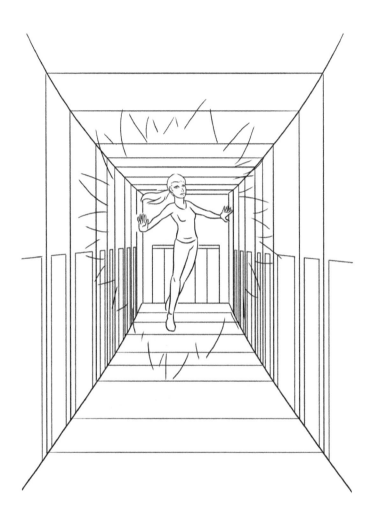

Back on the sixty-seventh floor, Jenna floated euphorically inside a glowing white-hot shield and watched the temperature slowly lower and the bright white light fade as she hung in the air feeling bedraggled and exhausted, but alive—more alive than she had ever felt in her entire existence. She stayed there for ten whole minutes until the glowing and temperature had normalised and then took another deep breath. She straightened her torso, opened her eyes, and prepared for her mission again, but this time with unrelenting confidence.

Jenna floated towards the lift door and immediately passed straight through it without any hesitation. She looked down in the darkness of the lift shaft and pushed out her hand. Light emanated from her palm, revealing the vast drop below. A sudden noise and rush of air made her jump as the lift came down from above and passed through her body. She caught a glimpse of two security guards travelling within the lift as it passed.

'*That was a weird sensation,*' she thought.

She flew downwards and caught up with the lift and passed into its cabin to float beside the guards. She watched the numbers count down on the lift display as they travelled. The guards were talking about a football match that had been on earlier in the evening and how the referee had made a bad call. The lift stopped on the ground floor, but this was not where she needed to be. She eyed the panel's buttons and could see several underground floors.

'*Where would they keep him? Where will I find him in this vast complex?*' she wondered.

'*In a cell,*' she answered her own question. '*And where would they keep a cell to hold a powerful monster? In the basement, as far away from everything else as they could go.*'

Jenna looked at the numbers on the panel again and could see that they went down to minus seven, but there was one after that labelled 'Sub-basement'.

'That's where he is.'

She passed through the floor of the lift effortlessly and plummeted with greater confidence down to where the lift shaft ended. The gap from the lower seventh floor to the 'sub-basement' was much larger than the other floors. As she passed through the lift door, she could immediately see why.

Jenna had entered an enormous underground hangar. It was big enough to house a jumbo jet and the vast high ceilings were lined with gargantuan steel beams to support the building above. The standard Darwinian white could be found everywhere, with fake sunshine being pumped in from lighting hidden within the ceiling beams. The wall she had walked through housed the only feature on the plain white concrete sides of the hanger. It looked like a control centre, one that NASA's mission control would have been proud of.

She entered deeper into the room and looked up to see thousands of computer monitors being viewed by Darwinians in black suits hustling and bustling about. The room overlooked the hanger from roughly sixty feet above ground level and was separated by a thick glass ceiling-to-floor window. Jenna presumed the glass was there to protect the inhabitants from whatever was going on in the main hanger. She turned to take in what they were monitoring and saw the sprawl of a clear white floor before her. The only interruption to the openness were groups of people in long black hooded cloaks standing perfectly still in circles, facing each other. There were five groups near mission control, and one larger group at the end. The circles were roughly thirty feet wide and the cloaked figures were lined up with mathematical perfection. She estimated that each circle was made up of seventy people, and one had two rows, but the furthest circle at the end of the hanger was made up of four rows of people.

'That's two hundred and forty people all standing still in a circle. How curious . . .' she mused, *'. . . what are they doing?'*

Jenna walked closer and noticed the large holes in the ground. The hanger was made up of twelve large holes, evenly spaced apart, in two rows of six. Mission control was directly looking over five holes with the cloaked figures around them. Then there were some empty ones and then the two at the end: one with four rows of people and the other with none. The cloaked figures were standing around the edges of the holes, which had dictated their perfect circles. As Jenna approached, she could see a thin metal rail around the empty holes that had been put in place to prevent people from falling in.

A massive bang made Jenna jump with fright. She looked up at mission control to gauge their reaction and could see them frantically running around. A few moved over to the glass, pointing and miming instructions to the people below. She followed their gaze to the hole with two rows of cloaked figures around it. The people were now extremely active, throwing their arms high and waving them around, casting all kinds of spells and curses down into the hole below. Another bang came, slightly louder than the first, and a few of the figures fell backwards onto the floor. The individuals around the other holes had tensed up, but were remaining perfectly still. A rush of movement made Jenna look to her right, where a double door had opened and more cloaked figures came rushing in to help the ones who had fallen and to make up a third row around the hole with the activity.

Jenna did not have to wonder about what they were so afraid of or what was making the noise. She had already realised that these holes were pits to hold ghost Warriors. They were designed to have no way in or out but the hole above, which was surrounded by Protectors shielding them from escape and punishing them into weakness. There were six pits with protectors around them. Jenna guessed the one now under special guard held James, who had been causing the bang she noticed back up on the sixty-seventh floor. The four pits beside him were likely for Gwion, Patrick, Grub, and Mark, and the one at the far end with four rows of Protectors had to be for the legendary Skinny. Jenna watched a single cloaked person walk out of the double doors and up to a circle, relieving one of the Protectors who marched back with exhaustion on his face. Jenna watched this happen several times over the course of five minutes and realised it was shift change time. She moved quickly to the double doors and traced the path back to the Protectors' robing room, which looked like a locker room from a high school. She tried several lockers, but they were all locked and looked too sturdy to break into.

'*You twit, Jenna,*' she berated herself.

She allowed her hand to pass through the first locker door and felt around inside. She could not feel what she was looking for, so she stuck her head in too. She withdrew from inside the locker and was holding one of the long black cloaks used by the Protectors. She put it on and materialised while staying clear of the other Protectors who were preparing themselves. Jenna followed a group of three out to the main hanger and became very nervous about being seen. She was now wondering if this was a good idea and second guessed her actions. She was torn between staying cloaked and flying over the pits at the risk of being detected by so many Protectors. Surely, they would feel her on their shields, especially now that she was emanating more power than ever.

Instead, she had chosen to disguise herself and would walk in amongst them and stand as one, so as to not interrupt their shields at all. As she walked closer, one of the three protectors ahead split off and started walking in the direction of Skinny's pit. She could feel her panic rise inside. Surely, she could escape this situation with her newfound power, but she could not escape with James or the others, and not even perhaps with her own children.

She watched with her hood down low—just enough to see out, but not enough for anyone to clearly see her face through. The Protector ahead approached the circle and paused. A hand was slightly raised in the circle and this was the signal for the swap. Jenna took a deep breath and walked towards where she hoped to find James. She paused and waited. A hand was raised on the far side facing mission control and she slowly and calmly walked over and swapped positions with a person in the front row. Jenna extended her hand out over the edge with her necklace wrapped around it as all the other Protectors had done with their elements. She paused for a second to prepare herself for what she may see and finally, with fear in her heart, she looked down.

Chapter 14: The Pit

The hole was roughly fifty feet deep and had been painted plain white throughout. Jenna's heart welled up for as her eyes reached the base of the pit she saw a wretched creature in poor condition. James sat breathing heavily on the floor of the hole. He was covered in cuts and bruises, some freshly opened, causing blood to trickle down his skin to the white floor. Jenna wanted to cry and held her breath to try and stop herself. She scanned the base of the pit and could see that the only other object in there was a black bucket for a toilet. There were red and yellow stains all over the floor from where the Protectors had beaten and wounded James, causing his blood to spill out as it had now. Judging by his terrible loss of weight, he had been starved and he looked ready to die. If he had been here for all the weeks she had been unconscious, then perhaps he was ready to do so and it was surprising that he had lasted this long. James stood slowly and the protectors around the pit tensed. He heaved and sagged around the base of the pit like a tired old lion ready for death. Then he held his hands high and slammed the wall.

BANG!

The whole hanger shook, and Jenna had to hold on to the rail to prevent herself from falling in. The protectors around the edge went into a frenzy and James cowered and crouched into a ball as streaks of light and flashes pelted his skin. He screamed as their spells landed.

Jenna wanted to cry even more now, and anger rose from within her. She threw a few spells down in the pit, missing his body by several feet, and waited for the calm. She knew what

191

needed to be done and this required complete silence. Within five minutes, they had stopped punishing James and he had decided to sit against a new section of the wall directly beneath Jenna. She focussed and slowly manifested a tiny particle of oak in her palm. She felt it spark into existence and allowed it to grow only to the size of a pea. She looked down at her poor husband and smiled at what was about to take place: pure and simple revenge.

James looked up at the blank and cold faces above him and wondered how much longer he could take this. He wondered if anyone had heard his explosions and after so many weeks and with no sign of help he despaired. He held his head with both hands and ran his fingers through his hair for comfort. As he sat on the floor of his cell, he wished only for the knowledge that his wife and children were safe.

A tiny plink on the floor next to him raised his alertness to the extreme and his hand moved to draw the new object into his palm with barely enough time for anyone above to notice. He felt its power and knew what it was before he looked, but the impossibility of it all meant that he must have a glimpse. He curled into a ball and held his hand tightly closed inside. James shielded it from the eyes gazing down with his head and opened his palm slightly. Within his palm, he could see a pea-sized piece of oak. James cried and whimpered with joy at being saved and glimpsed upwards to find the source of his salvation. He immediately saw the necklace and one tearful eye from within the hood of the cloaked figure, and then he smiled as he steeled himself for what was about to happen.

James stood up and wandered to the middle of the pit, focussing his energy once again into his arms and drawing it into the oak within his palm. It grew quickly, and James used the focussed energy to draw water in from the surrounding air to rehydrate himself. He stretched his torn body and flexed his ragged muscles as the water vapour came to him and then he began to focus on healing. He was careful not to reveal the oak in his palm and restricted its growth so it stayed hidden. James regenerated and healed with every passing minute. Fifty feet above him, Jenna could hear the concern from the whispers around her and someone had alerted mission control. The figures there were now huddling at the window and watching James, discussing how he was doing this.

Ten minutes had passed, and James was starting to resemble his old self, but now with more scars than even before. He stood still in the centre of the pit with his arms outstretched and legs a few feet apart, absorbing all the energy he could draw in as his body grew. He felt his open wounds close up and then he knew it was time to let the anger in.

The oak in his palm started to grow from either side of his closed fist until it began to resemble his deadly staff that he would use to punish the Protectors above and all Darwinians from this moment on. James grew quickly in size. His muscles bulged and his skin turned bright red, then his eyes became black. His tail whipped around in anger whilst the rest of his body stayed perfectly still. Panic grew immediately and the signal was given to rain unrelenting attack down on him. Protectors from the surrounding pits were instructed to reinforce their numbers immediately. The first few blasts hit James' skin, but were stopped from doing further damage by his own shield. James roared up at the Protectors, flexing his enormous body and revealing his long sharp yellow fangs. He looked so fierce that some of the Protectors above whimpered and faltered momentarily. Jenna had waited for this moment to reveal her power and cast an incredibly powerful shield over her husband below.

Everyone in the room felt the enormity of the power that was just cast and James froze, feeling its glow wash over him. He looked down over his body and knew that they could no longer touch him. Jenna, still hidden beneath her cloak, walked away. A few frightened Protectors called out to her.

'Come back! Where are you going?'

She was only twenty feet away from them when she cloaked herself and was gone from their sight in an instant.

The protectors above James were throwing every terror they had at him, but nothing got through. He roared again, louder than ever before, and the Darwinians in mission control went into overdrive.

The Protectors above James were suddenly sucked into the hole they had been trying to keep him in, as if a giant vacuum cleaner had been turned on. There was a second's pause before a giant explosion announced the reign of chaos and all the Protectors were flung out of the pit in a cloud of fire and black smoke. Some flew high in the air and others smashed against the high ceiling. An alarm started shrieking and red lights flashed. The ground between the first two pits exploded as if a knife had swiped at it from below. It was James wielding his staff, carving the ground away to reveal a path to whomever was next to him. James looked through the gap at the limp and weakened frame of Gwion, who held his hand aloft with his palm facing outwards.

'Weapon!' he cried.

James manifested the tiniest amount of iron ore in his hand and threw it at Gwion. It looked like James had thrown nothing, but Gwion's Warrior senses picked it out and caught it with tremendous speed and dexterity. James knew that, like himself, that was all he needed. He crouched down and then jumped out of the pit.

Darwinians started streaming in from all sides, and they were no longer just Protectors now. Instead, all kinds of wizards entered the area. Each one was determined to bring down the great Ghost Warriors, but none of them could penetrate the shield Jenna had created. James seized the moment and sent forwards five giant blasts of energy that burned and catapulted the attacking Darwinians all about the hanger and shattered the glass to mission control.

James turned and peered down at Gwion, who was healing and growing with every second and then he manifested elements for Grub, Patrick, and Mark, throwing them down to the wretched creatures they had become. A new wave of Darwinians entered the hanger, but their efforts would be futile. James spun his staff high like a helicopter, charging it with power before releasing it in a broad sweep across the face of the approaching enemy. The Darwinians had enough time to throw devastating curses and spells at James, he remained unharmed and started striding towards Skinny's pit. As he approached, the Protectors that were stationed around Skinny panicked.

'Stay back!' someone called.

'Stay back or we will attack you!'

James laughed at this and the deep thunderous sound coming from the belly of a twenty-foot tall, bright red, black-eyed, muscle-bound devil with a dragon tail was enough to frighten a few of the Protectors into retreating, causing even more panic amongst those who stayed. James left the few who ran past him as attacking a fleeing enemy was not the ghost Warrior way.

The fleeing Protectors who managed to get past James were even more terrified to run past the four new devil Warriors who had just leapt out of their pits, wild with anger and slaughtering anything that dare to attack them. The Warriors reaped carnage on the Protectors who got past James, making those who were left—roughly one hundred and fifty cowering wizards—realise that they were penned in at the back of the hanger with no escape.

Jenna watched from the hidden depths of the hanger and warned the Warriors silently of the enemy numbers gathering in the wings, but each one of the Warriors by now had felt the newfound power of Jenna's shield and all concerns of attack were disregarded in arrogance. This moment, for them, was all about taking revenge on those Darwinians brave enough to fight.

James looked down at the peaceful, statuesque figure of Skinny, who sat cross-legged and looked deep in meditation. He appeared to be unharmed in the centre of his cell. James manifested a tiny amount of ivory and tossed it down to the floor before him. Skinny moved his hand towards the splinter and pressed his index finger on it. He did not move an inch, but the splinter grew at an incredible speed into a long white samurai sword. Skinny slowly gripped the handle, rose to his feet without the use of his hands, and morphed into the jet-black devil ghost Warrior of legend. He leapt out of the pit with ease and landed before James. They eyed each other for a moment until Skinny reached out a giant hand and swiped James around the head. James roared into Skinny's face so hard that it ruffled his yellow hair and spit flew out through his wide open mouth past his long fangs to land on Skinny's face. Skinny did not react. His massive frame stood perfectly still, waiting for James to finish his display of power.

'You bang too much. Skinny not slept for many days!' he bellowed.

A silent signal from Jenna told them of the approaching masses in the hallways and James looked beyond Skinny at the cowering Protectors who had been penned in.

'You deal with them. We will take the next wave,' he rumbled.

Skinny calmly turned to see his captures cowering before him. He let an evil smile stretch across his face and approached.

'Warriors, steady, approach on my flank,' came James's instruction.

Mark, Gwion, Grub and Patrick happily turned to face the oncoming enemy. They wished to cause more carnage on those who had dared to capture and torture them. As they approached the oncoming masses streaming into the hanger, they heard the roar of Skinny shouting 'Boooooo!' behind them followed by the stampede of the retreating Protectors that were penned in running past. Skinny lined up next to James and looked at him.

'They not fighters,' Skinny said with a half giggle on his lips.

'Figures,' replied James.

The stampede from the fleeing Protectors caused the incoming front lines of Darwinians to falter and retreat, the ones that stood their ground had the monsters tear into them, brandishing spells and curses and ultimately wielding death. The Warriors thought nothing of danger as they were at this moment completely untouchable under the protection of Jenna's immense power.

Chapter 15: Hadrian's Revenge

Jenna floated high above the hanger floor and watched her husband and his comrades reap revenge against those who had captured her family. She was eager to go and get her children, but knew that the Warriors needed to teach the Darwinians a lesson. She hoped that it was one that would make them think twice about coming after her family again. As she watched from a great height, she felt an old, familiar, and unwanted presence enter the hanger. She could feel Hadrian's power and arrogance, but it did not feel quite right.

Jenna looked about for the distinctive bowler hat for a few minutes and then saw Hadrian standing where the glass had been high up in mission control. He was watching the giant devils tear into his people with a grimace on his face and anger in his eyes. His tall wiry frame stood upright and tense and he had both fists clenched. He drew his hand back in the air and opened his palm as if he was about to throw a pitch in a baseball match and a large blue ball immediately materialised in a swirl of electricity. Jenna could feel the enormity of his power on her shields even at that distance and could not believe her own feelings. She shook herself awake from the shock and watched as he threw it towards Gwion.

'*Gwion, duck!*' Jenna screamed in his head.

The blue energy ball zoomed past Gwion's head, missing it by a few millimetres, and hit the ground some fifteen feet behind him. The explosion was enormous and it shook the building far beyond the rumblings James's had created. Everyone on the hanger floor flew backwards from its place of impact. For a few seconds, there was complete silence. Jenna knew immediately what had happened as this was no ordinary power that Hadrian now wielded: it was her son's. Gripped tight in Hadrian's left hand was a tiny bright blue rock that had recently been sapping Rafi's power up on the sixty-seventh floor and now it was clear why.

The Warriors and Darwinians picked themselves up in a daze and Hadrian drew his arm back, preparing another devastating blow. Jenna looked at the hate in his eyes and could see it was directed towards James. She flew down to float just ahead of James and positioned herself between the two men. Hadrian loosed his spell with a scream and the blue ball flew directly towards Jenna. She drew in her power and pushed it into her shield with all her strength. The impact was immense, and to Jenna it felt like she was trying to stop a freight train with her bare hands. The drain made her materialise and fly back towards James, who caught her in his arms before the explosion reached him, and the two of them flew back and landed on the floor. Jenna was safely cocooned in James's giant frame, but they were both on their feet instantly. Whilst the explosion was immense, it appeared that the rest of the hanger was unaffected as Jenna's shield had absorbed most of the explosion. She looked up at Hadrian, who was snarling from the window frame high above them.

'You!' he pointed at Jenna. 'I knew you would be a nuisance. I should have left you at the Lost City where we found you!' he called out.

James heaved his great weight towards Hadrian and roared.

'Your time is up, Hadrian,' he snarled.

'Ha! How wonderfully fitting that the power that kills you both will be that of your own son.' Hadrian held aloft the blue glowing rock in his fingers and laughed. Then he gripped it tight, threw his hand back again, and formed a much larger blue energy ball. As it swelled in his palm, blue lightning flashed in from the ceiling to his hand. As the lightning struck his palm, the ball grew faster until it was the size of a person.

'*Can you stop this one?*' James spoke in Jenna's head.

'*I think so, but hold tight,*' she replied.

'Oh, you think you can stop the power of an Olympian, do you?' Hadrian had somehow been listening to them. 'Well, how about the power of twenty Olympians?' he called out.

A sudden rush of Darwinians came up behind Hadrian in mission control, overlooking Jenna, the bewildered Warriors, and the still bodies of hundreds of black-suited Darwinians spread out over the floor of the hanger.

James looked at Jenna and she gave a look back of despair, knowing fully well that her newfound power could never hold back the power of twenty Olympians. James held his staff vertically with one hand and raised it high in the air. He charged it with as much power as he could. Skinny, seeing the move he was about to make, charged his samurai sword with energy and leaned the tip over to gently touch James's staff, causing a greater rush of energy. James slammed down his staff to the floor, releasing an impressive spell directed towards Hadrian. A great crack appeared at the base of the staff and opened up at breakneck speed, heading towards mission control. It was like a fault line was opening up before them. As the crack disappeared at the base of the wall where mission control was housed, Hadrian smirked at their last attempt to avoid death.

'Is that all you have!' he bellowed. 'You missed.'

The hanger went silent.

'Did I?' James called back.

There was a slow creaking sound, and suddenly, the wall housing for mission control split down the middle, causing the room within it to burst apart and crumble before them. Hadrian screamed as the ground gave way and threw the energy ball, but in his panic, his aim was too high and it hit the far wall of the hanger, causing a devastating blast that made everyone fly forwards through the air. The Warriors somersaulted and James once again caught Jenna and hulked his body over hers to protect her from the debris. The building started to rumble and some of the overhead gigantic supporting beams came away and crashed down around them.

'I think the building is coming down!' Jenna screamed over the loud rumbling.

'Let's get the children and go,' called out James. 'Meet you back at your place.' He had directed the last comment towards Gwion and the rest of the Warriors.

'We finish this together!' Gwion called back.

'Aye!' shouted the rest of the Warriors.

One of the massive beams crashed very close to them and they jumped.

'Let's go,' said James.

Jenna floated up only a few feet off the ground and passed through the doors to the hanger where she had first entered, heading towards the elevators. The Warriors all stood still for a moment, stunned at what they had just seen her do. She stuck only her head back through the double doors.

'Come on then. What are you waiting for?' she called.

She pulled her head back through and went off towards the lifts again. In the hanger, the Warriors all looked at James.

'I didn't know she could do that,' he said in awe.

'Let's go!' called Skinny, avoiding a large piece of concrete, and his massive bulk burst through the double doors, taking away a large part of the surrounding concrete, too. The other Warriors' giant bodies followed through the larger hole. They found Jenna beckoning them towards the doors to the lift.

'Follow me,' she called out and disappeared through the doors.

'Her doing that is starting to freak me out,' came Mark's deep rumbling voice.

Jenna travelled up the lift shaft, letting out light beneath her for the Warriors to follow through the palm of her hands. A massive crash below signalled they had entered the shaft and she looked down to see Skinny and the others leaping, bounding, and clawing on the shaft walls like giant spiders tearing up behind her.

She sped up and reached the sixty-seventh floor just a couple of seconds before Skinny tore another giant hole in the lift doors for them to come out of. The building was shaking and shuddering violently now, and they knew it would not be long before it fell.

'Down here.' Jenna headed towards the dormitory.

As she reached the door, she passed through it and then stopped in her tracks. At the far end of the room stood Renee with her three children. All the others had gone, presumably having been evacuated, but there they were before her, looking terrified. Renee held her arm outstretched in front of her with a shiny short black wand in her hand. In an instant, three black ropes grew from the tip, flew out, and wrapped themselves around the children's throats.

'Get back or else!' Renee screamed.

Jenna froze and the room was void of all noise, bar the rumbling of the faulting building as it strained to stay upright. An implosion of the wall directly behind Jenna signified the entrance of Skinny and the rest of the devil Warriors. They stood behind her like something from a horror movie, with their chests heaving as they sucked in vast amounts of air to replenish themselves from their climb. Fear was written all over Renee's face.

'Stay back!' she screamed again.

James moved in closer.

'Don't come any closer!'

James stretched his giant hand out and a small pulse of white light emanated from his palm. The ropes burst into ash and Renee's wand flew out from her hand, darted across the room, and embedded itself in the far wall across the corridor with a twang, like an arrow hitting its target.

Jenna reached her hands out and the children ran into her embrace. Renee stood frozen with fear and wore a look of complete horror.

'Ghosts have honour!' she blurted out. 'Ghosts don't harm unarmed wizards!' she shrieked whilst cowering under James's slow approach.

James sighed and turned to look at Jenna.

'She's right,' came his low rumble.

Jenna stepped in close to Renee, so close that they were practically touching.

'There is no such code for Protectors,' she whispered in her ear.

Renee twisted her head and looked into Jenna's eyes. What she saw must have terrified her because she started muttering incoherently and raised her hands to protect herself.

There was a large burst of white lightning between the women, and the Warriors held their hands up to shield their eyes. They missed Renee's departure from the building through the window behind her. Jenna turned and saw the sorrow in her daughter's eyes, and without hesitation, darted to the remains of the window and held her hand out. Light pulsed from her palm and she visibly relaxed. She turned to her daughter and beckoned her over. Jenna picked her up and pointed to a distant person far down below on the street outside who stood dazed and confused. Saskia recognised Renee and felt relief that her mother hadn't killed an unarmed person. They turned to each other and Jenna kissed her forehead.

'Thank you for helping to stop a terrible mistake' she said to her big blue-eyed daughter.

Jenna placed Saskia down on the floor and closed in on all her children again.

'Let's get out of this place,' she called out over the continuous rumble of the building as it started to tip into a full collapse. A white mist rose up from the floor and swirled around the six giants, three children, and Jenna, and with ten pops, they were gone.

Chapter 16: The Stronghold of Atlantis

Nellie stood in her kitchen baking yet another cake. She baked when she was nervous, and over the past eight weeks she had been very nervous indeed, not knowing where her husband and sons were or how they were doing. She felt their arrival and immediately ran outside to see the swirling white mist in the sky above her house. Then she heard a distinctive pop and tried to count how many people there were.

The ten figures high above Gwion's house were huddled in a big group. As they floated down gently, they all caught their breaths and the Warriors shrank down to their human forms once again.

Nellie ran into Gwion's arms and he held her tight. From somewhere within Gwion's big frame came her voice.

'I was so worried!' she sobbed.

'We're ok,' Gwion whispered. 'It was close, but we are ok.'

'But bloody hungry, Mum,' said Grub loudly.

Everyone started laughing and Nellie ushered them in to eat. All ten of them sat around the kitchen table, feasting on the goodies Nellie had baked whilst she cooked a sumptuous meal in a variety of cooking pots. As she went about the kitchen, they filled her in on the events that had happened.

'What's next?' Nellie asked Jenna.

'I don't know. Where can we go? We will never be safe from them. My parents knew that and now I do, too. They want our power, and they will do anything to get it,' replied Jenna.

'Why do they want our power, Mummy?' asked Saskia whilst stuffing a cupcake into her mouth.

'Because it's a power struggle,' answered James. 'They are the most powerful wizarding organisation in the world. They do not want to share their great power when they can simply take yours and become even greater.'

Zachary and Rafi had stopped and listened to the answer. The children shrugged, seemed to accept this as making sense, and carried on eating.

'I think your hopes lie with the League of Olympians,' Nellie continued. 'Their whole organisation is based around the idea that the Olympians will return to Earth one day and lead the world once again. And here you are.' She smiled.

'I think she's right,' Jenna said to James.

'You wouldn't even have to find them. Mark could take you to them. Couldn't you, my love?' Nellie directed her question towards Mark.

'Normally, the League is kept hidden from the world. Their location is a guarded secret, but in this case I think they will make an exception. After all, I would be bringing them four Olympians,' said Mark.

'Four? You mean three,' said Gwion with a mouthful of meat.

'No, I mean four.' He looked at Jenna.

'How do you know?' asked Jenna.

'You were a "whisper", travelling through doors and walls without the slightest effort. You shielded six devil Warriors deep in the throes of battle without the slightest attack reaching us. I felt the power coming from your shield. You are no ordinary wizard, Jenna.'

Jenna described her own Dawn back on the sixty-seventh floor and the realisation that her parents had known what she was. James sat still with his mouth hanging wide open and a look of complete shock on his face. Jenna reached out her hand and rested one finger on his chin, closing his mouth for him.

'Can we stay here?' asked Rafi.

'Maybe for one night.' Jenna looked at Nellie.

'It's too dangerous, my love. They will come here looking for you.'

'She's right,' said James. 'We need to find the League of Olympians. They will welcome us and offer us protection. Mark, will you help?'

'Do you even need to ask, old friend?' Mark placed his big arm around James. 'This is just another one of our adventures.'

'I'm coming with you,' said Gwion firmly.

'And us,' said Patrick, looking at Grub, who nodded.

'No!' snapped Nellie. 'Can't I have you for a few days? You can join them soon. I just want you for a few days here, safe with me. Mark will tell us where you are going, won't you, my love?'

'Who says we are safe? You heard what they did to us!' Gwion snapped back.

'That's because you were with them. If you stay, it will be just us here again!' Nellie strained to put a weak smile on her face and rested her hand tenderly on Gwion's shoulder.

'Skinny is going with you.' These were the only words Skinny had spoken since arriving at the house.

'And we are too!' Gwion snapped back, slamming his hand down on the table. 'Warriors stick together. We are family, Nellie.'

'So are we, my love.' She held his face in her tiny hands.

'It's already decided,' he said, looking down and avoiding her gaze.

'Well, I will wait here and pray for your safe return,' Nellie said with tears streaming down her face and ran out the room.

Gwion sat still and looked down at his feet.

'Gwion, go to her,' said James. 'She is right. Who are we to put your family in danger? Me, Skinny and Mark can handle this. Plus we now have the ultimate Protector—an actual Olympian.' James reached out and squeezed Jenna's hand.

'No! I will have no more talk of this!' Gwion shouted. 'Who are we if not family? We are ghost Warriors, and we have looked after each other for centuries. When they came after the Cyclopes, hunting us like animals, you were there for me. When the world turned on wizards and all magic, we fought back together. How can you ask me to turn my back on my family now?'

'Ok, ok, calm down. I'm sorry,' James said quietly.

'We are in this together.' Gwion looked at his sons and they nodded.

'Thank you,' said Jenna.

'Right. Now, young Mark Anthony, where is this secret organisation based?' asked Gwion.

'You're gonna love this,' Mark replied and smiled.

Gwion and Nellie hugged tightly and kissed deeply before he let her go and stood with the group in the small English-style garden deep in the surrounding jungle.

'Where are you going, Mark?' Nellie asked. 'In case I need to send help.'

'It's best you don't know, Nell. It puts you in danger,' he replied.

'And if they come for me, where will I go for help?'

'Nellie, I can't tell you. Secrecy is all we have to stay safe.'

'Well! There's only one thing for it then. I'm coming too!'

'What? No!' snapped Gwion. 'You stay here, where it's safe. It could get rough.'

'You said it yourself! Who says it's so safe here? It wasn't exactly safe at the rodeo, was it?'

There was an awkward silence as everyone contemplated the argument before them.

'Right then. Give me a minute,' said Nellie, walking back into the house. She emerged two minutes later with a large pink canvas bag over her shoulder. 'Just a few bits,' she stated to the group. 'Let's go, young Mark.'

'Right, Jenna, take us here.' Mark closed his eyes and sent over their destination silently.

'You have to be kidding,' Jenna responded.

'Trust me.'

'What? Where are we going?' asked James.

'Here we go,' Jenna said with a smile.

White mist swirled up from the ground and the eleven figures disappeared.

They reappeared into darkness, high in a dark turbulent sky. The wind whipped them around, a flash of lightning lit up their surroundings, and thunder clapped. There was no land anywhere in sight, only the sea chopping about violently beneath, threatening to reach them with giant waves.

'Mummy!' screamed Saskia. 'I'm scared.'

James held the children tightly against his body,

'Don't worry, I've got you!' he called out to them over the noise of the wind and rain.

'You're up,' Jenna called to Mark.

Mark took out his large emerald green broadsword from the sheath fastened to his back and held it in both hands with the tip pointing downwards towards the sea below. He focussed for a moment and then a burst of white light pulsed from the sword and travelled down to hit the surface of the sea, where the light spread out and was immediately absorbed. The sea continued to swell violently beneath them and the storm blew. Everyone watched the sea where the energy had hit it.

'Nothing happened!' Jenna called out.

'Oh, ye of little faith,' Mark called back.

A few more seconds passed, and slowly the sea directly beneath them started to swirl in one direction. The swirl was about two hundred feet in diameter and steadily got faster and faster until the group huddled together high above could see a giant whirlpool start to form. The whirlpool turned ever faster and deepened as its speed increased. Slowly, a vortex opened up beneath them. The whirlpool made the already violent and vast ocean look even more terrifying. The mouth of the vortex grew to over one thousand feet and its depth disappeared into the darkness, forming a giant, mouth-like tunnel that led to the deepest parts of the ocean.

'Jesus! I'm not going down there,' said Gwion.

'You afraid?' teased Mark.

'You bet your life I am. Cyclopes don't swim.'

'I never knew that,' said James.

'Well, it's not something that I shout about.'

Mark moved his broadsword to point down into the vortex and let another blast go. The group watched the ball of light travel into the mouth and then sink deeper and deeper, lighting the way as it travelled. It continued on for a very long time and was a mere speck in the distance when it flashed slightly brighter and turned into a green light before disappearing.

'It's ready!' called out Mark.

'Well, I'm not,' replied Gwion.

'Don't worry, Gwi, I've got you!' Jenna shouted above the noise of the storm and the ocean.

She held her hand high and let it fall slowly with her palm outwards. The group could feel Jenna's powerful shield come down over them and the opaque blue glow of its presence disappeared with her final movement.

'Feel better now, you big chicken?' Mark called to Gwion.

'Oh shut up!' replied Gwion. Nellie giggled, which made everyone laugh except Gwion, who frowned. 'Come on then. Let's get on with it!' he shouted.

Mark nodded to Jenna and she led them down into the mouth of the vortex.

'Faster,' called out Mark.

She moved the group floating in her shield down at an extremely fast pace and darkness fell upon them quickly. Mark, Gwion, and Grub pushed bright white light out of their elements and hands to light the way and everyone stared in awe at the wall of water swirling all around them. Its enormity gave only the slightest clue of its true power, but it was enough to hypnotise those travelling within it.

'I see the bottom!' called out Zachary.

Everyone looked down, and in the far distance was the grey rock of the ocean floor. Jenna sped them up and they quickly closed in on it. She slowed them down at the last second and they touched down on the wet grey rock. The open area was about fifty feet across and consisted of large grey jagged rocks, deep canyons and cracks in the ocean floor. Jenna looked up and could no longer see the top of the vortex, making her feel nervous.

'Now, what?' called out Nellie.

'Now, we go in.' Mark smiled. He turned and walked around the side of a large wet boulder and out of sight. Everyone followed him curiously with their necks craning out in front of them to get a glimpse of where he was heading. Behind the boulder was a large natural crack in the ocean floor where the rocks within had formed a rough and slippery staircase. The group entered a cold, wet, jagged cave that looked unfriendly and destitute. Jenna looked at Mark and he smiled again, held his hand out before him, gestured over to the far wall in the darkest part of the cave, and pushed out light from his palm.

'Blimey!' said Rafi.

The cave in the darkness opened up to twice the height in the far end, where a large archway had been delicately carved into the rock. It was like the centrepiece of an exhibition in a museum. The sides had carved mermaids draped around winding sea serpents with mermen riding their dragon-like heads. The sculpture became more glorious as it led up to the top, where the largest figure, a muscle-bound man leaning over the entrance, stood poised with a long three-headed spear pointing down at anyone passing underneath. The figure was a giant compared to the other mermen and mermaids and he had a long beard that whipped down and around him.

'Poseidon,' whispered Nellie.

'Yep,' answered Mark. 'Welcome to the stronghold of Atlantis.'

Mark walked through the arch and lit the way to an incredible staircase that wound down into a larger and more elaborately carved cave beneath them. The grouped walked in with their mouths hanging open. As they walked down the winding staircase, they could see incredible giant carvings on the walls depicting life in Atlantis and stories from Greek mythology.

'Look! It's a Cyclops,' called out Saskia to Gwion.

'So it is,' he said quietly, taking in the sculpture of a Cyclops battling a two-headed dog.

The staircase ended at one end of a large, cathedral-like cave complete with vaulted ceilings. It took the group a few minutes to descend to the floor. Once at its base, they had to walk the full length of the hallway to the opposite end, where two colossal doors stood sealed from the rest of the world. The carvings on the ceiling and around the main doors depicted all the gods of Olympus, with Poseidon at the end on one of the doors, standing roughly one hundred and fifty feet high and looking down scarily at anyone wishing to enter.

'Who's that on the other door?' asked Zachary.

On the matching giant door from Poseidon was a similar-looking giant holding a jagged-looking rod.

'Zeus, the King of the gods,' answered Mark. 'He is Poseidon's older brother.'

'These two great wizards are our ancestors, kids,' Jenna told her children and pointed to the two giants staring down at them.

Everyone stopped and took in what had just been said.

'I prefer Grandma and Grandpa,' said Rafi, making everyone laugh.

'I don't fancy my chances at opening these doors. How about you, Skinny?' called out James.

Skinny laughed and shook his head.

'These doors have not been opened for many centuries,' said Mark. 'We are using the tradesmen's entrance,' and he tipped his head in the direction of the corner of the hall. Mark walked over to a carving of a snarling dog. This was the corner piece of the giant relief that had the two doors holding Poseidon and Zeus at its centre. The dog stood about twenty feet high, with his large head hung low and a massive mouth with long sharp teeth before them. Mark walked past the massive protruding head and approached the body, which was mainly within the wall. There was no sign of an entrance of any kind.

'You sure about this?' asked James, who was holding his wooden staff at full length in battle position.

Mark looked about and noticed the other Warriors had their elements in attack readiness, too.

'Easy boys, he's just a statue,' laughed Mark. 'Just don't pull his tail too hard, then he might bite.'

Mark grabbed the thick tail that curled out from the wall and hung his entire weight on it. The sound of stone scraping against stone signified something was moving, and with a little wiggle from Mark, who was now hanging in the air, the tail moved down slightly. There was the clear sound of a click. Immediately, the dog's head moved and shook itself to life. The head looked about, as if the dog had been woken in anger. He barked a loud whooping bark that made everyone jump.

'You have to be kidding!' shouted James.

The dog focussed on him and snarled.

'Easy boy, easy. Don't shout. He doesn't like loud noises, do you, boy?' Mark was speaking to the giant dog like it was a baby. He walked around the massive head and tickled the dog under his chin. 'You like that, don't you? You like Uncle Mark.' Mark turned to the group. 'He's just a pup and he loves a bit of attention.' Mark rubbed and tickled the enormous stone head and the dog whimpered and licked him. 'Come on, boy, open up. Let us in,' called out Mark, with a final tickle behind the dog's ear.

The dog stretched his mouth open wide and froze again. His tongue was the last thing to move and slowly flicked itself into a small staircase that led into his body and deep inside the wall. The group once again stood frozen with their mouths open.

'I don't think this could get any weirder,' said Saskia under her breath.

'You're not kidding. This time last month I was in my science class,' replied Zack. 'And now, oh look! Here I go into the mouth of a giant dog, several thousand feet underwater, in the lost city of Atlantis, with a bunch of wizards.'

Jenna shot a worried look at James.

'Come on, you lot. There is nothing strange about any of this. It's a perfectly normal day for anyone.' James chuckled as he followed Mark down the staircase and into yet another cave. The group all entered into a small cubed room with perfectly smooth stone walls that stood about twenty feet high and twenty feet across. At the far end was a round entrance filled with a large cylindrical piece of stone. The entrance was the full height and width of the room and was shaped into a perfect circle. The cylindrical stone rock blocking the passage filled it completely. It had a flat face with the outline of Poseidon's three-headed spear imprinted into its centre.

'That's funny,' said Mark.

'What could possibly be funny about this?' said Saskia to Zachary.

Mark looked at James awkwardly.

'What?' asked James.

'Well, the entrance to Atlantis . . . .'

'Yes, where is it?' James asked impatiently 'So far, we've gone down the vortex, through the hidden passage, past the archway, into the great hall, and through the stone dog—what now?'

'That's just it. Now, we're supposed to go in, but the entrance is blocked. I don't understand it. This is the entrance, but it's got this big rock blocking it.' Mark tapped the big cylindrical rock held within the entrance.

There was silence within the group for a few minutes until James rolled up his sleeves and headed towards the rock.

'Right then,' he said, patting it with his hand. 'Doesn't look so tough to me.'

Skinny moved forward.

'I have destroyed much bigger rocks before,' he pitched in.

James looked about and the Warriors stepped forward.

'It's a baby rock where I come from!' Gwion said and laughed along with his sons.

'Best stand back,' Mark called to Nellie, Jenna, and the children, who moved back to where they had entered the room. The Warriors surrounded the stone blocking their path and charged up their elements with power. Gwion was the first to strike with his massive blue mallet and rock flew out on both sides of him. As he moved his mallet away, Skinny sliced in with his sword and more chunks of rock flew out. They had already removed a massive section.

'This shouldn't take too long,' Mark mouthed to Jenna over the noise of Grub and Patrick, who were throwing their weight into it.

Lastly, James threw the tip of his staff into a gouge made by Patrick and a flash of light pulsed upon impact. The rock burst apart, revealing nothing but more rocks behind it. The Warriors paused for a moment to assess the damage they had caused and Nellie moved closer to get a better look.

The rock started to glimmer and sparkle all over, slightly at first, and then the sparkling grew faster and brighter.

'Stand back!' Gwion called to Nellie.

'Jenna,' James called out to his wife.

Jenna recognized her cue and cast a shield over the group quickly, just in case.

The Warriors took a few steps back as the rock seemed to come alive, pulse with light and sparkle. There was one final bright pulse of light and everyone shielded their eyes. When the light died down, the rock was whole again and all the fragments blown away from it had disappeared.

'Well, it is a fortress,' Mark stated with a touch of embarrassment at not being able to get in.

The Warriors went to work again, faster this time, in hopes of reaching the other side before the rock could heal itself, but the rock had been activated and every blow was healed before the next one could hit. All the men stopped, having made no marks or dents, and breathed heavily from their efforts.

'It is a blocking stone,' said Skinny.

'Yeah, it sure is,' piped up Grub.

'No! Blocking stones are made from very strong magic,' Skinny continued, 'nothing gets through, ever!'

'Brilliant,' Zachary muttered under his breath to his sister.

'There must be a way,' Jenna said to Skinny.

'Blocking stone disappears after test is passed,' he answered.

'What test?' asked James.

'Test different for all blocking stones.' Skinny shrugged.

Jenna and Nellie approached the stone. They examined it and then looked around at the Warriors, who looked back blankly.

'Anyone got any ideas?' Jenna asked the group.

'Maybe there's a clue somewhere,' Nellie suggested and everyone started looking around the room. The only feature on the smooth plain stone walls of the square room was the blocking stone and the three-headed spear embossed on its flat face.

'What about the trident?' Jenna said, placing her hand on the outline of the three-headed spear.

'Is that what it's called?' asked Saskia.

'Yes, it was Poseidon's wand and element, so perhaps he cast this spell here.'

Rafi wandered into the centre of the room and looked about, but no one paid any attention to this. He held his little hand up towards the walls and turned around in a slow circle, waving his palm before him. A fine mist of water started to seep in through the surrounding rock and everyone stood still, watching the little wizard silently. Slowly, the mist built up before him into floating droplets, which connected up to make large bubbles of water, all moving and wobbling around in the air directly in front of his little form.

Rafi raised his other hand and placed both of them together with his arms outstretched and closed his eyes. The bubbles of water all joined up to make a large floating blob that quickly stretched out horizontally at his chest height, with a bulbous bit at one end that branched out to grow three heads. Then it was obvious that Rafi had made a large trident out of water, which was floating and moving in the air before him. He moved his right hand out, still with his eyes closed, and waved it underneath the trident. It immediately froze solid and turned white. He raised his small hand up and grabbed it in the middle, turning it vertically before bringing it to his side and opening his eyes.

'Cool!' said Saskia.

Rafi looked at her and smiled and then he looked at his mother. The little boy moved forwards towards the blocking stone and placed the trident into the embossed imprint of the same shape at the end of the rock. It was a perfect fit. Rafi closed his eyes once more and the trident glowed blue with his power. It pulsed with light three times, and on the third attempt, the light was so intense everyone shielded their eyes again. When they opened them and moved their hands away, the rock was gone.

Chapter 17: Homecoming

'Welcome, young Rafi, to the city of your greatest grandfather,' came the strong voice of an old man at the far end of the tunnel that was the entrance to Atlantis.

Only his silhouette could be seen as there was a bright glow of light from behind him. The group all wandered forwards, led by Rafi, and James quickly caught up to him and grabbed his hand.

'You have nothing to fear here, James. You are amongst friends,' came the voice again, echoing off the tunnel walls. 'We are the League of Olympians, and you have ended our wait for their return by bringing four Olympians into our brotherhood. Welcome Zachary, welcome Saskia, welcome Rafi, and welcome Jenna. We have been waiting a long, long time for you to arrive.'

As they approached the end of the tunnel, the man standing there came into view. He was tall, lean, and very old looking, but without any signs of frailty. He stood leaning on a chrome staff that narrowed down to a sharp tip and had a bulbous, jagged, round head that he leaned both hands on as he propped his weight on it. His skin was pale and wrinkly and his hair was pure white all over, right down to his long beard that he had plaited. He had wrapped the end of the beard around the top of his pole, leaving a length to hang down in the middle. The man wore a smart light grey three-piece suit, complete with a matching heavy hooded cape that draped all around him. A chrome pocket watch jutted out from his waistcoat and was attached to a chain that stretched over to his other side.

'I am Rufus, Chief Wizard of the League of Olympians and one of the world's oldest ghosts. Up until two minutes ago, I was the oldest ghost here.' He winked at Skinny.

Skinny's face stretched into a broad smile and he walked forwards and embraced Rufus in a giant hug that made him disappear from view.

'We have much to discuss,' said Skinny.

'I know,' muttered Rufus. 'There is much to do,' he replied with a stern look on his face.

'Let me welcome you to the ancient stronghold of Atlantis.' Rufus moved aside and waved his hand out in a gesture that guided their eyes to the city before them.

It was vast and beyond anything anyone could have imagined. The rough ceiling of the main cave soared over a thousand feet above, with small cloud formations and light pouring in from somewhere, while its sides were too far away to be seen. Up high, birds flew around a giant waterfall that allowed millions of gallons of water in through an enormous hole in the ceiling of the cave. The hole had more incredible carvings of Poseidon around it and was so perfectly formed that the water coming through was a solid stream and did not break apart as it gushed into a lake that sat in the middle of the city and fed canals travelling out in every direction. The canals wove in between incredible buildings that were Greek in style, but so modern looking that they could have been built today. Each building sat in a small, perfectly formed garden and was surrounded by trees, flowers, canals, and small tunnel entrances with more carvings around them. The city looked lush with greenery everywhere. The clean, strong architecture decorated with gold and silver made the city sparkle and glint from all angles. In the distance, where the rings of canals seemed to end, they became long straight veins that fed water out into vast fields and forests.

'Where's the light and heat coming from?' asked Zachary.

'This place has many enchantments left to us by your greatest grandfather. The light and heat come from the cave ceiling, but there's no visible source. See? You cast no shadow,' answered Rufus.

Everyone looked about themselves on the floor for a shadow, but none could be seen.

'Awesome!' said Rafi.

'Awesome indeed, young Rafi,' said Rufus. 'What did you think of Caesar, your great grandfather's dog?' He gestured back through the tunnel.

'Scary, at first, but I really liked him.'

'Excellent, excellent,' Rufus chuckled.

'Who are they?' asked Jenna, pointing at the other side of the great doors they had seen in the grand hall before entering the city.

The doors on the inside of the city were very different. They were gold and silver with edges that depicted a group of children in different scenes of play. The centre held the same group of children smiling and looking down on the great city. It was a massive sculpture of pure happiness and joy compared to the other side, which had clearly been designed to bring fear to anyone approaching the gates.

'They are the Gods of Olympus, but depicted as children. Many of them were brought up here and played amongst the buildings, gardens and forests. It was a happy time for them and probably the reason they chose to shield and protect Atlantis from the world above. Atlantis used to be an island directly above where we are now, but in a fit of rage Poseidon pulled the city underwater, to rest here for all eternity.'

Jenna was staring at the children in the sculptures and then back at her own children.

'The resemblance is unmistakable, is it not?' whispered Rufus.

It was true. Her three children were depicted within the group to an almost perfect match.

'The child to the left of Zeus in the centre is Apollo, god of music, poetry and knowledge, amongst others things. His resemblance to young Zachary is unmistakable.'

Everyone had stopped looking around the city and started listening to the conversation.

'The child directly in front of him with the golden hair is Aphrodite, goddess of love and beauty,' continued Rufus.

'She looks like me,' said Saskia with a big smile.

'That's me next to the boy in the middle,' piped up Rafi.

'Yes, young man. That child is Poseidon, god of the sea, earthquakes, and storms. See how he holds the three-headed spear known as a . . .'

'. . . Trident!' Rafi shouted, holding his up.

'Yes, indeed,' chuckled Rufus, ruffling Rafi's hair.

'Who is the child sitting at the very front?' asked Jenna.

'Looks familiar does she?'

'Yes, a little—actually, a lot.'

'Jenna, she looks like a photo of you as a kid,' said James.

'That is Athena, goddess of wisdom, warfare and intelligence, amongst others,' said Rufus. 'Interestingly she was known as a shrewd companion of the heroes, protecting those on heroic endeavours.' Rufus smiled broadly as he shared this last piece of information.

'Astonishing!' Gwion muttered under his breath.

The ground started to quake gently around the platform they were standing on, which overlooked the city. This broke the group from the spell of staring at the massive relief of the children on the doors. James and the Warriors jumped and encircled the children, except for Mark, who rested a hand on James's shoulder.

'Easy brothers,' he said.

'How rude I have been,' said Rufus. 'Allow me to introduce the League's council. We make up the twelve seats that lead our brotherhood and include some of the oldest living ghosts, although not exclusively the only ghosts in the League—we have many.' He winked at Mark. 'These individuals have played a part in keeping us hidden and safe over the centuries from warmongers, mankind, and the latest evil to face us, the Darwinians.'

Rufus turned around and looked down towards an open space just beyond the platform to where the sprawling city began. A giant carving of overlapping circles was imprinted in an expanse of marble, making it look like an elaborate mathematical shape. The ground started to quake much harder and a large crack appeared through the centre of the carving. Suddenly, the crack gaped open as if an invisible giant was tearing at it. The opening revealed a cavernous drop that could have reached the centre of the earth, but the view was obscured by thousands of giant vines twisting and turning as they pushed the gap apart further and further, coiling around each other with life of their very own. Eventually, the vines stopped twisting, the ground stopped shaking and the giant gash in the earth stood motionless. One vine prized itself away from the wall, and at its tip, three beautiful women stood still upon a massive leaf in long flowing dresses of bright colours. The leaf swung up from the hole and positioned itself next to the platform. The first woman, who wore a white flowing toga, had long blond hair that swept all around her. The middle woman, who wore a bright blue toga, had dead straight jet black hair that she had platted together and wrapped several times around her body all the way down to her waist. The last woman, who wore a bright yellow toga, had bright red wiry hair that stuck out from all angles at an incredible length making her body look tiny. All three women wore sandals and looked as though they belonged in ancient Greece.

Rufus turned back to the group with a smirk on his face and said 'allow me to introduce you. Meet Pippa, Hera, and Iliana: our war council'

'Secretaries of defence please, Rufus' said Hera in a heavy posh British accent.

'We have been attempting to modernise the brotherhood into more appropriate departments and titles,' said Pippa, the blond lady. 'Though some of us find it harder to modernise than others,' she motioned her head towards Rufus and the three women giggled.

'War council' blurted Grub. 'But they're all women?' he continued quizzically.

'You have much to learn about which is the more dangerous gender, son,' said Gwion, laughing and nudging him. Everyone giggled at this.

Rufus faced Grub and looked at him with a stern face. 'These ladies are all descended from Sirens. As dangerous as they are beautiful. You would do well to remember that young man.' He raised an eyebrow at him and turned back to the women.

'Because you called us beautiful, I'll let the dangerous bit slide, Rufus.' said Iliana in a thick Greek accent and a smirk on her face.

Rafi walked over to the edge of the platform and looked down into the abyss of vines.

'How deep is that?' he asked whilst being careful not to lean over the edge too far.

'That is one of many entrances around the world to the ancient gardens of Arcadia, an unspoilt wilderness beyond the reach of mankind where many of our magical friends live and practice magic.' Rufus said. 'Its depth, you ask? Almost to the centre of the earth, my boy'

'Awesome,' said Rafi looking down to view the base of the chasm before him. He glimpsed movement far below, seeing a bright orange vein near the bottom. 'Is that Lava down there?' he turned to face Rufus with a look of excitement. Rufus turned away to look at Hera with an awkward expression on his face.

'Perhaps.' He said softly. 'Ahhh there you are.' Rufus said in relief of the moment and turned to face an elderly bald man with a kind face and deep worry lines on his forehead, wearing a smart brown suit. The man reached the top of the staircase that led down to the city and turned to look up at the clouds high above. Immediately, a smaller cloud broke away and came swooping down. As the cloud came closer, it started to evaporate, and in the mist a teenage girl started to appear. There was a clear buzzing noise around her, and as the remnants of the cloud disappeared altogether, she stood at the very edge of the platform and a blur appeared from behind her. The buzzing slowed and two dark small wings that were beating almost faster than sight began to slow until they came to a standstill.

She withdrew them and walked gently over to the elderly man and joined arms with him.

'Meet David and Maryanne, our recruiters. They search the globe for like-minded wizards and magical creatures to join our ranks. David is the only non-magical member of the council, but one of many in our organisation. Maryanne is actually Queen of the Harpies, who recently joined our plight and delightfully inhabit the cloud formations within our city.' Rufus looked up and waved his arm towards the impossibly high ceiling where thick clouds formed. 'Ironically, history knows the Harpies as winged spirits whose name literally means "that which snatches".' He chuckled

'We no longer snatch.' Maryanne snapped and then calmly faced the group 'we are now the secretaries of promotion and recruitment.' She turned to the three Sirens and gently bowed.

The sound of sliding and scraping rock made everyone turn towards the tunnel the group had come through to enter the city. Next to the entrance, the smooth rock had split into large squares that were sliding apart and over each other as if the wall itself had become a giant sliding puzzle. The squares started speeding up and overlapping one another faster and faster, spreading across an ever-increasing expanse of the wall. The anomaly grew and stretched, and giant squares of different sizes pushed out and slid away to reveal more of the same overlapping and sliding. The spectacle increased until it became so large that the ground started shaking once again and the children moved in closer to their parents.

'Do not fear' Rufus shouted above the noise. 'He is nearly here.'

'Who is nearly here?' shouted James.

Suddenly, the wall stopped dead and the silence across the city was deafening. The group watched the centre of the wall fall away to reveal a monstrous sight. An incredibly muscular man with a bull's head was standing in a square recess in the middle of the wall. The figure crouched slowly and then sprung up with tremendous speed, leaping towards the group on the platform. Everyone anticipated the landing and quickly moved outwards. The creature landed on one knee with a giant boom with his head facing downwards and hands flat on the ground to steady himself.

'I am Asterion.' came the deep growl of the creature before them. He raised his head and looked at the group. 'I am charged with carrying out the punishment of those who defy the legion.'

'But his title is secretary of justice and punishment,' announced Hera.

Asterion huffed and puffs of steam came from his large nose.

'Quite' jittered Rufus, who seemed a bit lost for words momentarily. 'Asterion is the last remaining Minotaur, and a formidable ally, as I am sure you would agree.' Rufus said as he looked around at the other members of the council, who all nodded in respect of Asterion's theatrical entrance and overwhelming presence.

A beam of light interrupted the moment, shot through the tunnel and started swirling the remains of the falling dust into a mini tornado. The light looked like golden electricity, bolting whilst spinning the dust into a tight channel that pulled together into a column no higher than 10 feet. The lightening stopped and a man heaving for breath leaned on the column he had just formed in as casual manner as he could muster with a large grin on his face. He was young and skinny, and he had a large top of bright blond hair that was still waving from the extreme speed he had just demonstrated.

'Impressive, huh.' The young man beamed as golden electricity shot out all around him in a pulse.

'This is Myrtilus, our political liaison, or secretary for foreign affairs I think' said Rufus looking over at Hera with an air of uncertainty.

Myrtilus flared with electricity again and disappeared, only to immediately re-appear directly next to Asterion, resting his arm up on one of the giant's massive shoulders as he looked at him.

'How you doin', buddy?' he beamed. 'My entrance was better than yours.' He bragged.

A deep chuckle came from Asterion, much to the surprise of the family.

Rufus announced 'I'd like you to meet my assistant, chief magical and sorcery analyst, Dr Hecatoncheires or Hector as he is commonly known.' Rufus lifted his staff and prodded it in the air when a bright light flashed, causing everyone to shield their eyes. Soon, a short, round man appeared beneath the tip of the staff, wearing a tightly fitted three-piece pin striped suit and bright red bow tie. He was facing the wrong way and clearly was taken by surprise at his sudden teleportation. The man turned to face the family and looked about in shock.

'Erm, hello,' he stuttered in a gentle high pitched voice 'Lovely to make your acquaintance.' He looked at Rufus a little unsure and started to straighten his hair with his hands. As he did this, another set of hands appeared from within his jacket and straightened his glasses and yet another pair stretched down from the same area and pulled his trousers up.

'CooOOOooool' said Rafi, stretching out the word.

'Erm, thank you' squeaked Hector.

'Finally, I believe you already know our combat generals.' Rufus gestured towards Mark.

'You said "experts". Who's the other one?' asked Zachary.

Skinny stepped forwards and stood next to Mark. James's mouth hung open.

'Skinny! But you never said anything!' he exclaimed.

'Skinny waited until you were ready to know,' answered Skinny in his deep rumble.

'Hirotomi Tsunemori was one of the League's founding members,' said Rufus proudly.

'You said there are twelve members on the council,' called out Saskia. 'But you introduced ten people, adding you makes eleven,' she said to Rufus.

'Wonderful, wonderful' exclaimed Rufus. 'You are such a good study young lady. Someone is missing.'

A head appeared at the back of the crowd, and as the person stepped forward, the crowd parted to reveal an incredibly tall, well-built and handsome young man in a crisp black suit and white shirt.

It was Gwion's turn to be shocked. He grabbed his sons on either side to steady himself.

'Nathaniel! How can it be?' he whispered.

'Hello, father,' replied the man in the suit.

'I watched you die in battle almost a hundred years ago. How are you here? Where have you been?'

'In hiding, father. I'm so sorry to have not been in touch, but you moved on so quickly and I was needed here. There is much work to be done.'

'He looks like a Darwinian,' said Rafi.

'That's because he is,' said Rufus with another infectious smile. 'In fact, he's not just any Darwinian, he is in Hadrian's elite team, which is slightly ironic as he is also my number two.'

Everyone looked shocked for a moment.

'How else do you think we track their movements and plans and have managed to keep watch over your lovely family?' Rufus directed the last comment at James.

'Well, I don't care how you got here or why you didn't contact me, but it's truly wonderful to see you, son.' Gwion said and flung his arms around Nathaniel, who returned the hug with equal feeling.

Jenna noticed Nellie fidgeting from one leg to the other and understood that Nathaniel was not her child. This greeting probably made her feel awkward.

A voice called out from behind the group, making everyone jump and turn around immediately.

'Well, isn't this touching?' came the serious and dark voice of Hadrian, who was standing in the mouth of the tunnel. 'Pity, I had such high hopes for you, young Nathan. Now, I understand how the League has always managed to be one step ahead of me!' he snarled. 'But I knew that if I stayed close enough to these children, they would lead me to my triumph.'

'And what is that?' asked Jenna.

'An audience with the League of course, and the added bonus of four actual, real-life Olympians—and at such a tender and fragile age.' He reached out a long arm and flicked his finger quickly under Rafi's chin.

Rafi moved back and hid behind Jenna's leg.

'Ha! Perfect, absolutely perfect. Don't look so angry, Rufus. You have waited a long time to get me on my own. Sorry to disappoint, but I thought to bring some reinforcements, just in case you all have a desire to continue living.' Hadrian laughed.

A stream of Darwinians started coming in from behind him. Each one had a hand clenched into a fist, and from inside their grip, a blue glow shone strong and true. Jenna knew it was one of the stones Hadrian had used to drain Rafi's power, and she screamed a warning to James and the other Warriors.

'That's right, Jenna. What better ending to the League and the returning Olympians than to be defeated by the power of Poseidon?'

The stream of Darwinians stopped and James guessed there were about two hundred individuals.

'Too many wizards, even for you,' spat Hadrian at James. 'Especially with the power of an Olympian, thanks to that lovely son of yours.'

'So that's your plan is it? Kill the League and my family and rule the world?' asked James.

'Not quite "rule"—govern with democracy and laws.'

'Who polices the policemen!' shouted Zachary.

'Silence!' shouted Hadrian. 'Children should be seen and not heard.'

'And all those elected officials and governments you work for, they know you're here to kill the League and three innocent children, do they?' asked Jenna.

'Once the threat to Darwinian Global has been eradicated, democracy will rule once again,' he replied. 'Sometimes, tough decisions have to be made on behalf of the greater good.'

He shot a look at Nellie. Jenna followed his gaze and looked at her.

'It was you!' Jenna said coldly.

'What—what are you saying?' Nellie stuttered.

'What are you saying?' Gwion stepped in front of Jenna with anger written on his face.

'I'm so sorry, Gwion, but its Nellie. She's a traitor.'

'Rubbish! She's no more a traitor than I am!' he shouted.

'I'm sorry to hurt you, but it makes perfect sense. When Nellie looked into my children back at your house, she was so frightened of their power. When the Darwinians first attacked us at the rodeo, she drew me away from the children. Now, here we are face-to-face with Hadrian once again and the only people who knew our location came here with us. Nellie only decided to come along when Mark would not divulge where we were going. She sold us out, Gwi.' She looked at Nellie.

'It's not true! It's not. Tell them Nell.' He turned to her and froze.

Nellie had tears running down her face and wore a look of sorrow.

'I'm sorry, my love,' she said to Gwion and moved to take his hand.

He quickly drew it back.

'What! No—Nellie, tell them it's not true!' he shouted whilst holding back tears.

'Mum! How could you?' said Grub.

'They tortured us, Mum,' Patrick interrupted, with a look of horror on his face.

'I didn't know that they would hurt you—I didn't!' she said, looking around at the others. 'Hadrian promised me he would hold you captive only,' she whimpered.

'But you're ok with them killing me and my babies, right?' asked Jenna.

'They are dangerous. You are dangerous. The Olympians had their time. If given another chance, they will rule the world with tyranny.'

'And you think he is better?'

'The needs of the many,' she said quietly and trailed off into a sob.

'Come, stand by my side and we will spare you as we agreed,' interrupted Hadrian.

'And my husband and boys?'

'Stand with us now!' shouted Hadrian at Nellie.

'My husband and sons,' she repeated.

'I am giving you your safety. Now, stand with us before I change my mind.'

'But you said you would take care of Gwion and the boys too.'

'And I will,' Hadrian said as an evil smile stretched across his face.

'We agreed that Darwinian Global would do what is right.'

'Who are you to decide what is right for Darwinian Global?' he spat at Nellie with pure venom in his voice. 'These people here are keeping the company from maintaining peace and balance in the world. They must all die.'

'No, that's not what we agreed!' she screamed at him.

'You are in no position to make any demands. Now, this is the last time I will extend this offer. Stand with us now.'

Nellie looked at the Warriors and then looked around at the children and Jenna. Jenna looked at her with hate in her eyes. Nellie tore her gaze away from such hatred and looked at Gwion. His face expressed the pain he had in his heart.

'I'm so sorry,' she said quietly.

'Enough!' shouted Hadrian. 'Stand with us now!'

Nellie looked at him and hung her head low, staring at her own feet. She shook her head slowly.

'I have made a terrible mistake,' she muttered.

'So did I.' Hadrian said cruelly, and his long thin black wand appeared in his hand suddenly, pointing at Nellie. 'I hate traitors,' he sneered at her.

A blast of light shot out the wand and into Nellie. She reached out her hand towards Gwion as her body started to turn to stone, beginning with her feet. It was over within two seconds, and as the tip of her head changed, her body exploded into a thousand pieces, making everyone crouch to shield themselves from the debris.

'Don't be too sad, Gwion, you will be with her very soon.' said Hadrian, raising his right hand in the air.

All the Darwinians raised their wands into attack position. The Warriors all flashed with light and grew into ghost devils with their weapons in hand. They surrounded Jenna and the children. Nathaniel was now an addition to their numbers. The rest of the council made a second inner circle. Jenna pulled on her power and thickened the shield, ready for the imminent attack.

Hadrian stretched another of his cruel smiles across his face.

'You are simply not strong enough,' he said, raising his wand higher and charging it with power, making it glow white at the tip.

An explosion hit Hadrian, sending him flying back twenty feet. Everyone in the group except Rufus and the council turned to see where it had come from. They could see a single wizard in a bright green shabby robe high above them with his wand charged for the next strike. As they looked at him, more League wizards of all shapes and sizes started appearing out of thin air. As they became visible, they cast powerful spells and enchantments at the Darwinians, forcing them to defend themselves. This handful of wizards turned into hundreds, and then thousands as the League of Olympians revealed their true numbers and attacked Hadrian and the Darwinians with everything they had. Some blasts got through their extreme power and sent the black suits flying and crashing around the great gold and marble steps that led into the city. Rufus caught Hadrian's eyes as he stood and defended himself against more blasts.

'Did you think we were here alone? Ha! You were always too arrogant,' Rufus shouted out over the noise.

Hadrian looked about at the thousands of attacking wizards and then at his people who were getting back into position after the surprise attack. He noted that none of them had been taken down due to their enhanced powers.

'My turn!' he shouted back. 'Darwinians, attack!' he screamed above the noise.

The people in the black suits all charged their wands and sent spells through the air, tearing through the hundreds of League members who were in their way and causing utter devastation in an instant.

Screams were followed by bodies falling from the sky that fell all about the Warriors and the group within. Instantly, it was obvious that this fight was greatly mismatched.

Hadrian was the first to hit the group with a large blue electric ball of energy that crashed into Jenna's shield. She was able to hold it off, having known it was coming, but Hadrian was quick to react and pulled in four others to hit them again with burst after burst. The Warriors threw everything they had, but they could only destroy oncoming manifestations or slightly deplete the power of the oncoming spells. The newest attacks crashed into the surrounding shields, weakening them with every passing second. Jenna started to breathe heavily as she passed more power to them, straining herself to keep the group safe.

'You have to go!' shouted James at Jenna over the noise of the explosions. 'Take the children and go. Become a "whisper". Can you do it?'

'I think so.' she called back, pushing her hands out before her to charge a weakened part of her shields.

'Go now!' called out Rufus. 'We will hold them off for your escape.'

'But you will all die!' Jenna called out.

'We're dead if you stay or go,' James shouted back. 'Save the children. There will be others out there that will find you and help with the kids.'

Jenna let a tear fall down her face.

'I love you my darling,' she called out.

'I love you too' said James.

Several giant blasts hit them and sent James and Gwion flying out of the circle.

'I'll be with you always, my babies,' James said from the floor, looking at his children all huddled around his wife. Now go!'

Jenna looked one last time at him and then cast her hand down over herself and disappeared into a 'whisper'. James and Gwion were on their feet and sending spells back, but they were doing so to no avail. They simply could not hurt the Darwinians.

Jenna had not released her shield over the group yet, as she could not bring herself to let them die, but the drain on her power in making herself and the three children 'whispers' had weakened her enough that some of the incoming attacks had started coming through. The council and the Warriors were getting swiped and cut all over.

Zachary looked about at the horror of the battlefield around him. The League members were being destroyed before his eyes. Though their numbers were in the thousands, the explosions and blasts coming from the line of black suits simply overpowered all their attacks. The League members were sending over manifestations of all kinds. The League created a giant eagle which swooped down, but was hit by a blue swirl, and disintegrated. Four black dragons and stone giants came out from the city, but all suffered the same fate.

Jenna and the children floated one hundred feet away from the group of Warriors and watched the horror. Jenna knew she should get away while she still could, but she also knew that if she did, she would be leaving the council and Warriors to an imminent death. She decided to hang on for as long as she could keep her children safe. Hadrian started focussing as much power as he could on the Warriors and Jenna strained ever more to keep them shielded, but their obvious cuts and open wounds showed Hadrian that he was getting through. He glanced up as his next explosion hit and looked directly into Jenna's face.

'*How is that possible? How can he see me?*' she thought.

'Over there!' Hadrian shouted as he threw another energy ball at the Warriors and then looked up at Jenna and the children.

Jenna strained to protect the Warriors and the League council. She realised that with each hit they took, her power became increasingly strained, making her and the children visible.

'Mummy!' screamed Saskia as a giant blue ball of electricity came zooming towards them.

Jenna braced herself for the impact and used her free hand to pull her children in close. The direct hit made the temperature go extremely hot inside the shield and left Jenna breathing heavily. Whilst she was distracted, the Darwinians continued to hit the Warriors, and Rafi watched as one of the twelve-foot tall Darwinians sent a strong spell at his father which crashed at his feet and sent him flying high through the air in an uncontrollable spin.

James landed on his back, revealing a heavy gash in his side that bled on the floor. The large Darwinian moved out of the line of black suits and flew up high, watching James and preparing for a death blow. Rafi screwed up his little face in horror and anger. He could barely bring himself to watch. James could do nothing but hold his hands out before himself in a feeble act of protection from the death spell. The large Darwinian charged his wand and blue energy glowed bright at its tip. He threw his arm back and . . . bang!

The Darwinian was hit by a massive blue thunder bolt that was unbearably loud and cracked with such force that the battle stopped momentarily. The large Darwinian screamed and turned to ash immediately. He was the first of their numbers to fall since the battle had begun. Everyone followed the line of the thunderbolt back to tiny Rafi, who was floating just ahead of his mother and siblings right before they faded back into invisibility. Zachary and Saskia heard the 'plink' of the blue stone that had just fallen from the sky and landed on the golden steps. Zachary looked at the stone lying there, charged with his little brother's power, and then he looked back at Saskia, who nodded.

'Let's do this,' she said. 'Rafi!' she called and the little boy looked around, unsure of whether he was about to be told off. 'Do that again, but this time, let's play a game. You have to get as many of those guys in black suits as possible with one hit. Got it?'

'Easy.' he said.

The Darwinians came back to life and started their wave of destruction again, shooting more giant energy blasts from all angles.

Saskia looked at Zachary. He nodded and shot out into flight, away from his mother.

'Zachary, come back!' Jenna screamed through her exhaustion.

She tried desperately to shield him, but knew that her depleted strength and his quick movements would mean her shield would be almost ineffective if he sustained a direct hit. Zachary twisted and turned in the air, bounced off wizards, and darted away from explosions to land squarely on the floor next to the tiny blue stone the large Darwinian had dropped. He picked it up and looked at the innocent-looking glow in his fingers. Then he glanced at his father, who was some forty feet away and getting to his feet. James was desperately darting around to avoid the fresh wave of spells and blasts.

'Dad!' Zachary shouted.

James looked over in fear immediately and Zachary threw the stone with such force that it sailed at James with only enough time for him to raise his hand slightly. The stone slammed into his palm with perfect accuracy. James looked at the stone in wonder and then at his son. He half smiled, but the smile drained from his face as soon as he saw the black suit come into focus behind Zachary with a charged wand in his hand. There was no time for James to do anything except watch the blast head towards his son, who turned to see the spell coming directly towards his face.

Zachary raised his hand to shield himself. His last thought was of a massive metal shield and then he braced himself for death. A flash of light came from Zachary's wooden wand and a massive square-shaped chrome shield appeared between him and the blast. The shield glowed bright yellow and reflected the blast back at double the speed of which it had come, hitting the black suit and making him explode on impact.

Zachary opened one eye to see the end of the explosion and then turned to look at his father, whose mouth was hanging wide open. Zachary smiled, winked, and then stood tall. Another two blasts came at him and he causally raised his wand without looking. It glowed yellow again and two giant circular chrome shields appeared in their path just beyond him. This time, they were more refined, with decorated edges and carvings of him and his family on their faces. Once they had reflected the blasts, they disappeared as quickly as they had come. A giant crack of lightning made everyone jump again and signified another hit from Rafi. This time, he hit two Darwinians in one shot.

'I got two!' he screeched with joy.

Two more stones fell from the sky and Zachary did not hesitate. He leapt up with incredible speed and agility, catching them, and in one smooth movement he sent them on another trajectory towards Skinny and Mark, calling out their names as he targeted them. The two devil Warriors stood still, holding the tiny blue rocks in their hands.

'What are you waiting for?' screamed Saskia. 'Use them!'

This woke the Warriors from the spell of the blue glow and they turned to strike back at the line of Darwinians in suits. This time, the Warriors' unexpected power caught the Darwinian lines by surprise. The Darwinians hit back at the three Warriors, who were all injured and dull with exhaustion. Zachary barely made it in time to protect them with his awesome shields.

'Do something!' he called out to Saskia.

She looked at him and shrugged. She didn't know what to do.

'You're a Healer—so heal!'

This idea that Saskia could help in the battle had not yet dawned on her, but she reacted immediately to Zachary's words. Saskia charged her glass wand and placed the tip on Jenna. There was a sudden gust of wind all about her and Jenna felt the energy rush through every fibre of her being. It was over in a few seconds, but she felt completely revitalised and the strongest she had ever been. She looked down at the little blonde head next to her and deep into her cherubic face and blue eyes.

'Go help the Warriors,' she said.

'Yes, Mummy.'

With that, Saskia flew into the air, somersaulting her way through the destruction just as Zachary had done. She landed next to Zachary, who was holding his wand up high and swinging it around, pushing out shields to prevent the Warriors and the League members from being hit. Saskia moved in so that she was back-to-back with him and delicately aimed her strikes. The first one went to her father. This time, she was casting her spell from distance and her wand glowed bright white. The spell floated through the air like a wisp of silver smoke that crept up on James. Just as it was about to reach him, the spell paused and then struck like a venomous snake. It healed James like it did Jenna and then it recoiled back into her wand. The entire process happened within a second. James stood tall and strong, while he flexed his enormous muscles, before looking down at the gash in his side to find it was no longer there. He realised that many of his deep battle scars had also disappeared. He looked over at his daughter and winked at her.

'Thank you,' he mouthed.

A shield appeared in front of his face, protecting him from a direct hit.

'Wake up, Dad!' called out Zachary.

James roared loudly and flew into a battle rage around the Warriors, bringing down many Darwinians with his son's power to enhance his own. Jenna flew in above them and decloaked herself. She pushed her revitalised shields around those who needed protection. Rafi gently floated down to stand with Zachary and Saskia, who made room for him, so that they all stood in a small circle facing outwards, using their incredible powers to change the course of the battle.

As the fighting raged around them, Zachary shielded everyone he could and manifested a flock of golden eagles to swoop down and pick up the blue glowing stones from the deceased Darwinians and redistributed them amongst the League members. Saskia cast healing spells and found that she could send an enchantment across the lines of Darwinians which moved like a light fog to sap their strength. Whilst all these actions took place, Rafi picked out his victims and sent thunderous bolts from his trident, turning them to ash in an instant. Jenna looked down from within the safety of her shield and tears formed in her eyes at the sight of her children fighting back.

The battle did not last long once the children began to fight, and soon there were only a few remaining Darwinians cowering away from the oncoming Warriors. Hadrian still stood in the middle of the tiny group screaming out instructions, but the fearsome sight of Asterion moving in ensured there was no one left to instruct and he stood alone. Hadrian sent out blasts and spells that were instantly blocked by Zachary's giant shields and a look of despair crept in over his face.

'It's over Hadrian. You've lost,' said Rufus calmly.

'Never!' Hadrian screamed as he threw his arm back to send another blast.

The electric blue energy ball flew out and a massive clap of thunder accompanied by one of Rafi's immense lightning bolts blew the ball to pieces. Myrtilus flared with golden electricity and disappeared in a flash. He snatched the blue stone from Hadrian's hand whilst he was stunned from the strike and re-appeared by Zachary's side. Hadrian cringed and cowered.

'No,' he whimpered, 'you had your time. This was my time—our time.' He looked at the line of bodies wearing black suits around him.

'Evil will never triumph over good. You picked the wrong side,' said Rufus.

A giant blue bolt of lightning headed towards Hadrian accompanied by a massive clap of thunder. It struck all around him without hitting, due to an egg-shaped invisible shield protecting him from the impact. Inside the shield, Hadrian cowered and looked about himself in wonder. The lightning and thunder struck twice more in succession, but the shield around him held. Everyone looked at Rafi and the trident aglow in his hand. Rafi looked at the trident and shook it as if it were malfunctioning.

'That's funny,' he muttered to himself and shot a couple more lightning bolts with such force that they shook the whole of Atlantis.

'Stop that at once, Rafael,' said Jenna sternly.

'But Mum!' he complained and struck again.

It became clear that it was Jenna who was shielding Hadrian from a horrid death.

Everyone was looking at her with confusion on their faces.

'The battle is over and it is one thing to allow my children to defend themselves from tyranny, but another completely different thing for them to kill in cold blood. I simply will not allow it.'

Another massive bolt of lightning hit Hadrian, and once again, he was protected.

'Rafael, you stop that this instant or you will be in big trouble,' warned Jenna whilst shooting a look at James for support.

James sighed and heaved his giant self to face Rafi. He stepped forwards and shrank down to his normal size. The surrounding Warriors followed suit. This relaxed the atmosphere in the group a little.

'Your mother is right. You must not kill this man, son. Your teaching must begin here and you must learn that killing in cold blood is wrong. Now, put down your weapon.'

'But Dad!' protested Rafi.

'But nothing,' said James harshly. 'Do it now.'

It was Rafi's turn to sigh, hunch his shoulders, and look down. As he did this, the trident glowed one last time and then melted into water and trickled away. Jenna pulled his little body towards her and held him tight.

'Well done, Rafi. I know you just want to help and save us and you have done that, you, your brother and sister won this battle and now you must learn the value of human life, even one as low as Hadrian must not be murdered in cold blood' she said.

'But he was mean to us!' sobbed Rafi into his mother.

'Well, I am not about to stand here and let this vermin live another moment,' said Rufus.

Jenna stood and faced him.

'I, of all people know the evil this man is, but surely if we kill him today in cold blood,' she turned to face the group, 'are we not as bad as he is?' she asked.

Rufus stepped closer to Hadrian and started to walk around him in a circle.

'You make an excellent point, my dear,' he said to Jenna. 'But let me compare your pain to that of many others. Take myself for instance. As a young boy, I was told that my Dawn was exceptionally powerful and that I was to become a great wizard. My parents and teachers watched me grow and strengthen until one day they feared my power and the life I may choose, so they called in a group of powerful and strong wizards to guide and teach me further. I became very close to one teacher in particular and we spent many years in each other's company, until one day he asked me to join them and watch over mankind and the wizarding world to police them. I was unsure if this was the right thing to do, so I refused, and they left. I was devastated, but I held fast to my decision.'

Rufus continued to calmly circle Hadrian whilst he talked.

'A few months later, I saw smoke in the distance as I walked home from school. I knew instantly that something terrible had happened and rushed to my parents' house, only to find a smoking crater where it used to be. They were gone and I was an orphan. A friend of my parents' helped me find my mentor, my teacher, and he welcomed me back with open arms and helped me find the killers of my family. These were renegade wizards, those who used their power for themselves and cared nothing for other creatures or the greater good. It was this lesson that changed my mind and I joined my teacher, policing wizards and mankind for many years. I was one of the founding fathers of Darwinian Global. Together we prevented this kind of killing from happening to many others as we punished wizards who stepped out of line.'

'We were strong, and we grew stronger every day with every recruit and every political ally. Then one day, I caught a glimpse of an idle thought in my mentor's head, and in a moment of weakness, I stretched my power to look deep into his mind, unbeknownst to him. There I found true horror—a psychopath who would stop at nothing to gain ever more power. It was then that I found out the true killer of my parents. It had been my mentor all along, and he had done it to trick me into joining his group because they needed me.' He paused and looked at Jenna. 'My mentor, my teacher, my parent's murderer, was Hadrian, and I have waited for his death for far too long.'

Jenna was shocked to hear such a horrendous story and looked deep into the pain in Rufus's eyes. Rufus could see Jenna's empathy and used this to seize the moment. He leapt in close to Hadrian and flung his body onto him, getting inside Jenna's shield. The head of his chrome staff glowed red and sharp spikes grew out of it to make it look like an ancient weapon. Rufus plunged the spikes into Hadrian's chest and he let out a scream. Jenna moved her hands to cover Rafi and Saskia's eyes and stared at Rufus, whose own eyes never broke her gaze until Hadrian's spoke his last words.

'You fool' he cried. 'You need me to battle him.' He raised his left arm and pointed limply towards the giant chasm beyond the platform.

Rufus turned to him and whispered in his ear 'Only good can defeat pure evil. Fighting evil with evil never allows the good to shine through.'

Rufus withdrew his staff and Hadrian's body heaved and fell to the floor dead. He stepped forward, holding his head high.

'And so ends the killing,' he said to the group.

Everyone was solemn for a moment and they all nodded.

'What did he mean, who is coming to battle?' demanded James

'The fires have come back,' Rufus said softly looking down into the chasm before them. 'This can only mean one thing. Another Olympian has come into the world and Hadrian sensed it, as did I only a few years ago. Those are the fires of Oceanus, the river that young Rafi spotted. It has been dormant for many centuries. It marks the edge of the underworld. A world ruled by. . .' he paused and looked at the group of people before him, 'Hades.' He said this name with fear in his voice.

'He is here on earth again, but he is young, like these Olympians, so time is on our side.' He turned to face James and Jenna 'This is why the League and Darwinians alike have searched and prayed for the other Olympians to return. That is why you must allow us to teach and train you for the greater good or mankind may once again become mere puppets of the gods.'

'What are you proposing you do with me and my children,' questioned Jenna, stepping towards Rufus, and holding his gaze with strength and concern.

'I suggest that right now it is time for a new era—one of peace and harmony, learning and wisdom,' said Rufus, looking at the children.

'But what of Darwinian Global? Will they still come after us?' said Jenna.

'I think I can help with that one,' came Nathaniel's voice from the edge of the group. Stepping forwards and straightening his black tie.

'By killing Hadrian, Rufus just gave me more power from within their ranks.' He stepped close to Jenna and placed a hand on her shoulder. 'I will try my hardest for the Darwinians to no longer be your enemy, but your friend,' he said and smiled.

Jenna rested her hand on his.

'Thank you so much,' she turned to the group, 'thank you all! And what of Hades?' she turned back to Rufus.

'Let us prepare and teach you here, in Atlantis,' pleaded Rufus.

'I noted there were no secretaries of education within your council,' Jenna turned to face Hera.

Hera spread her arms open and gestured to the whole group.

'We are all teachers and carers for the Olympians, my dear.' She said with love in her voice 'It is our very purpose. For one day, you will protect and teach us.'

'Go back to your home and your life Jenna,' Rufus interjected, 'allow the children to love and respect mankind, but come here every week to learn and train, is all I ask.'

Jenna turned to James and they both nodded in silence.

'Yes of course,' she said, taking James's hand in her own.

'Yes and thanks to you all,' said James, stepping to stand beside her. He turned to his wife. 'What now?' he asked facing her.

'Now,' she paused and looked about at her children and then back into her husband's eyes, 'now, we go home.'

The End

Continue reading the next
book in the series.....

HIDDEN MAGIC - The Truth of Merlin the Magical

Christmas at the Rockefeller Centre, New York City was always a magical time. Families were out skating while people are bustling around the streets doing last-minute shopping and pausing to watch the festivities. A large choir of children began to sing the magical 'Carol of the Bells' somewhere within the hubbub of the flags, decorations and shoppers.

The throngs of people in the streets and on the ice paused and listened as the classical piece captivates them with the feeling of Christmas.

A woman in the crowd with a long hooded cape tore herself away from the spectacle of the children singing and looked up. She could feel something was there, but yet no one could see it. She moved out from the crowd of people coming in closer to hear the choir singing louder and louder. The woman raised her hand palm out towards the sky and let it fall before her face to reveal what she feared. High above them, something was pulsing and generating an immense golden domed shield around the people below, shielding them from the magic within so that they could carry on their Christmas joy oblivious to what was happening within their midst.

Hera pulled down her hood and stared at the peak of the dome, where she could see a single person. It was Jenna Bradbourne, focussed and determined. One hand was stretched out behind her powering and pulsing the shield and the other was facing downwards, controlling something below.

A giant red tail whipped in the air and the tremendous vibration of a large object hitting the floor ran through Hera.

She looked about to see if anyone around her noticed, but no one did. Hera frowned and stood on her tiptoes to see above the heads around her to what was beneath Jenna. People were in her way, so she moved further out the crowd, risking exposure. She moved slowly at first, unsure if it was the choir peaking once again or her feeling of woe and despair at what she might see that made her move faster. She began to run for a clear view of the monster being tormented below Jenna.

Hera burst free from the edges of the crowd and bumped into a man in a heavy winter coat and scarf. He turned to see her rush past as his shoulder pushed out from where she collided with him.

'Hey lady, watch where you're going.' He cried.

Hera didn't look back. She stayed focussed on the area below Jenna: a vast open space where she finally saw him clearly. James was in his devil Warrior form, but his size and additional strength could not help him now. Hera watched in despair as James thrashed around in agony and leapt up towards his wife. Just as he was about to be within reach, an invisible force pulsed next to Jenna and he was flung like a rag doll down to the earth again, slamming into the concrete and writhing in pain.

Hera looked about. Her keen senses picked out others hidden in corners, watching the spectacle. Some were horrified and desperate, while others seemed to be enjoying the show.

'Asterion!' Hera calls in her head.

A giant man with a square shaped head walked up beside her.

'I am here.' came Asterion's deep voice.

'Tell the generals they must take action immediately, but to be cautious, this is a trap' Hera continued out loud.

The human form of Asterion walked away and a golden lightening blur stopped him in his tracks as Myrtilus arrived to stand before him.

'The children are here!' he whispered desperately.

'Make sure they don't see their father. That is your task, Myrtilus' said Asterion.

'On it.' And with that, Myrtilus bolted from view.

Nathaniel walked out of the New York subway nearby in his black suit, white shirt and black tie. He looked about casually and then flickered as if his body were being re-tuned to an old TV show. His attire became that of a New York policeman. He turned to face the subway exit below and tilted his head to the side, indicating to whoever was in there that they could come out. Mark, Gwion, Patrick and Grub emerged in their human forms, shortly followed by Zachary, Saskia and Rafi. Skinny was the last out and glanced back into the tunnel to check all was clear. The party approached Nathaniel at the top of the stairs.

'Careful, it's icy.' He called down.

The children's eyes ran everywhere as they had never been to New York City before, but a blur of golden electricity returned their focus to their mission as Myrtilus appeared before Nathaniel and whispered in his ear. After a short conversation, Nathaniel nodded and Myrtilus bolted away. Nathaniel turned to the group.

'Saddle up.' He called, pointing his truncheon upwards as if it were a wand.

There was a pulse of light that the passers-by could not see and the children watched a large light blue half dome cover them all.

'Stand back,' said Skinny to the children as Nathaniel beckoned them over.

Once out of the way, each one of the Warriors flashed in turn and became bulging, muscular, horrifying devil Warriors and Cyclopes. Rafi thought to himself that he wished he could do that and he heard a voice in his head.

'One day, you will be the biggest of us all,' came Skinny's voice.

Rafi looked at the terrifying monster that was now Skinny, and the giant Warrior winked at him and then looked off in the direction of the Rockefeller centre.

Nathaniel and the children walked through the crowded streets, whilst the Warriors leapt and clung to the buildings, making their way without crushing anything or anyone. All five Warriors clung in a line down the corner of Rockefeller Plaza, which sat on the square to the ice rink. They hung like primitive apes in a tree, one under the other, but the tree was a skyscraper and the apes were the monsters of legends and nightmares. At the base of the column, Grub looked down at Nathaniel who immediately stopped in his tracks and halted the children.

'What is it?' said Zachary

'You can go no further, we must wait here.' replied Nathaniel.

'Why, what is it?'

Nathaniel looked at him and frowned.

'We have found your parents,' he said softly, 'but it's a trap.'

'Where are they?' Rafi exclaimed with excitement, tiptoeing to see over the people.

'They are cloaked, over there.' Nathaniel pointed in the direction where he could see James writhing around like a wild dragon fighting invisible enemies.

'I want to see my mummy and daddy.' Called out Rafi.

Nathaniel crouched down to be eye level with the children.

'We need you here for your power,' he said gently, 'but it is best you do not see what is happening unless you have to.'

'Are they ok?' asked Zachary.

'No, they aren't I'm afraid.' replied Nathaniel and he stood and looked up.

Rafi's little head looked down to the floor. He felt someone watching him and raised his head slightly until he noticed a small boy across the road from him, standing between a man and a woman, holding their hands. The family were very smartly dressed in fine clothes, but old-fashioned as if from the 1920s. The little boy was plump and his slick oiled hair was combed over to one side. The parents were staring at Rafi with cold, hard faces, as was the little boy. The plump boy took his hand from his mother and waved it palm out in-front of him towards the children. Rafi heard a giant thud, which made him and the other children jump. Zachary and Saskia turned to see the horror of their father being tormented by their mother in the distance, but Rafi remained focussed on the little plump boy, who broke into a wide smile and took a short, Shakespearian bow.

The little boy's eyes flared red, and then both his parents' eyes followed suit shortly after. They all began to laugh at him in a giggle and then slowly into a roaring howl. Rafi felt tremendous anger and turned to Nathaniel sharply.

'Who is that?' he gestured to the boy across the road.

Nathaniel tore his gaze from James writhing around and looked to where Rafi pointed.

'Who is what?' he said.

The little boy and his parents had disappeared. Rafi turned again to look at Nathaniel and then caught a glimpse of someone flying high above them in the distance with a powerful shield projecting down below. He focussed his eyes with a squint and recognised his mother.

'Mummy!' he cried out and flew upwards.

Nathaniel reached for him in a scramble as he flew past, but missed and took off after Rafi.

'Stay there, out of sight.' He called back to the other children in a panic.

Rafi paused in mid-flight, causing Nathaniel to crash into him in a tumble. In the distance, a man wearing a light green, three piece tweed suit and matching top hat materialized directly next to Jenna. He had bright red hair and matching pointy beard, and he held a long white cane with a chrome round top in his hand. He was jutting it to the beat of the choir far below. With each pronounced prod of the cane came a pulse of white light down on the leaping and roaring figure of James beneath him.

The monstrous red giant leapt high again and stretched, but this time a giant shackle materialised on his leg and pulled him back to the ground violently. James roared and the man in the top hat laughed and then looked over at Rafi and Nathaniel tumbling some distance away. He extended his cane and shot a bolt of energy towards them. Just as it was about to make a direct hit, Skinny leapt into its path. The bolt knocked him out the air and onto the ground nearby with giant thud. Jenna looked over at Rafi and her eyes flared with gold, then she looked back and re-focussed on containing the monster far below her.

The man in the tweed suit waved his cane high, and a beam of light pulsed upwards towards the sky.

The children noticed tiny dark figures started flying in from distant hiding places all around the square and then four giant thuds around them signalled that the devil Warriors had taken flank about their position.

'The trap is set,' called out Nathaniel, 'Get them out of here.' he cried to the Warriors.

Pippa appeared with a pop and white mist and waved her wand high. All three children felt the cold around their feet and could see mist swirl all around them. Just as the world became a blur and disappeared from view, they could hear someone shouting.

'He's back, it's Merlin!'

Then for the children, there was silence.

To Be Continued...

About the Author

Born in Central London, England on the 29th April 1974. N.D. Rabin grew up in a loving home in North West London dreaming about a day when he would use his imagination to make his children and others smile at the thought of the impossible.

Follow me (N.D.Rabin) or ask questions on the following links:
· https://www.facebook.com/NDRabin/
· https://twitter.com/Neilrltd

Thank you for inspiring this book and my love goes out to the following people:

· My parents (Philippa and John) for being strong, encouraging and a constant source of inspiration

· Michael and Caroline. Thank you for always being there and so strong through our turmoil

· Maryan for standing by me through thick and thin, I will always love you and you will be forever in my heart

· My fellow Brat Packers. Thank you for being so supportive, funny and immature with me. Our friendship is so strong and yet immature on equal measures

· J for many years of peace and happiness. I will always cherish those years in my heart

· Jon and Amy. Thank you for being supportive throughout my time writing this book and long before it was even started. I look forward to many more years of our friendship

· **Finally and by no means the least, 'My three little twinkles'. You are the reason for this book and a constant source of love and joy to me. Thank you my babies**

Lightning Source UK Ltd.
Milton Keynes UK
UKHW041858191222
414174UK00002B/263

9 781524 676773